The

1002nd

Book

to

Read

Before

You

Die

Contents

Legal Disclaimer:

The Scottish Arts Council strongly repudiate all the claims made in this novel.

THE BIRTH OF
THE READER

I

"Lizzie MacDonald, allow me to insert a fact-filled eclair into that whining piehole of yours. My name is Marcus Terence Schott. Upon the cessation of this phone call, I will be leaving this office for a period longer than Neptune takes to orbit the sun. So I can, without fear of an interdepartmental probe, impart this sliver of real into those burning aural canals of yours: flee the country. Pack your possessions in two suitcases, kiss your dependants farewell, and bum the boulevards of Haussmann, slum the streets of Kurfürstendamm, pound the pavements of Greater Nuuk. Your existence is being eaten and the eater is E-Z-Moneee Loans. In two weeks, five brainless ex-bouncers with sold souls will plunder the place you call home, lifting everything from that lost paperclip under the settee to that soiled cloth crumpled in the attic corner. Your existence now belongs to the Boumount Financial Corporation, of whom we are a subsidiary, and at the tick of a box, you will be conscripted into our white slave trade initiative, packing boxes in a Greenock warehouse until arthritis renders your usefulness null, and you are dropped into our retirement prison, where nurses will dope your soup, leaving you to drool insensate in front of *Bargain Hunt* until death. Lizzie: leave. You have a chance, if you leave now, in two seconds, when I put the phone—"

Marcus terminated his career on £12,200 per annum as Senior Loan Advisor at E-Z Moneee Loans. In the staff room, office manager Geraldine Hum and line manager Hannah Sharp stood in linen skirts over a table with two custard slices and a card capturing a sad chimpanzee's thought: "Sorry You are Leaving." Geraldine Hum was the lone worker whose natural enthusiasm for ensuring customers were salved in their sorrows before being shafted by the Senior Debt Collectors upstairs made the eight-hour shifts less like slavery, and for the third time, Marcus felt her warm tentacles wrapped around his skeletal frame, the pleasant heft of her bosom against his shoulders, and the consoling waft of her supermarket perfume, and for the third time felt a curious mix of maternal comfort and instant arousal. Hannah Sharp, as line manager, offered her compulsory parting handshake and insincere wish of a pleasant future in whatever field he had chosen to conduct this future. Once the pleasantries had concluded, she handed him a legal summons for damages to caller Lizzie MacDonald.

2

MARCUS SCHOTT was shot. Too long serving succour to suckers, sitting with wrist cramp on a plastic chair explaining the intricacies of an asset-based loan structure to semi-illiterates attempting to shout themselves into liquidity. Too long having his words shorn into short koans on loans, mangled in management meetings and parroted down the line verbatim under the listening ears of seniors. His passion was reading. Like most sane human beings, his true calling was sitting in a vacant room with the blinds drawn in a comfortable chair reading text running from left to right, verso to recto, for hours at a time. As a Senior Loan Advisor, his reading time had dwindled from five to one hour per day, sometimes dwindling further to a mere half-an-hour or fifteen-minute drowse in bed. The exhausting monotony, exhausting in its monotony, had exhausted him to monotony, leaving his limbs too weak to turn the pages, his brain too mushed to process paragraphs, his eyes too weary to permit life.

During his time in unemployment, he had honed his concentration to expert levels, reading from morning to late evening, sometimes two books per stretch: from the masterful biographies of Richard Ellmann, the riveting moral riddles of J.M. Coetzee, the laudable efforts of Louise Wener, to the mordant chuckles of Curtis White, the unflinching tales of Primo Levi, the toenail clippings of Nicholson Baker. Having completed three hundred books, the inevitable bane of a power-reader's existence arrived: loneliness, twinned with thoughts that life might be able to offer some of the delights featured in those books. He signed up for mild socialising at a book club, and in stepped Sandra Acer.

This luminous woman, six foot zero and small of face, brought the music of The Bats into his bedroom and the pleasant sensation of lips on skin spanning from forehead to pinkie-toe. The snug tent of a long-term union based on mutual love erased the need for Faulkner's complete works. The arching of her shoulders upon arising from bed annihilated the need for Gore Vidal. The hum of her soft skin in the morning light expunged the need for Charles Dickens. The patter of her feet outside his flat door torpedoed the need for Isaac Asimov. The rustle of her crisp packet at lunch nixed the need for Christopher Hitchens. The plop of her turds into the bowl vanquished the need for Boris Vian. He had swapped the sufferings of mankind in book after book for the care and attention of a long-legged woman with four GSCEs from the East Renfrewshire area.

Soon, Sandra Acer wanted progress. Marcus liked composing nonsense haikus in his pants while chugging down ciders. He liked eating chicken linguini and hugging her until her spine protested. He liked taking short walks around the same park and making the same derisive remarks about dogwalkers. He liked falling asleep on the sofa and waking up sucking the cushion. He liked to have his hoovering technique criticised on a rug-by-rug basis on Sunday afternoons. To appease her and find peace, he applied for a position at E-Z Moneee, and to his profound sorrow, was accepted at once. This solution proved futile, for the couple had become trapped in conversations of this nature:

"You are in love with being-in-love with me. You have no real-time love for me."

"I accept that I want to retain that being-in-love love we had from the beginning. But what is wrong with wanting that being-in-love love in place of the real-time love: a watered down version of being-in-love?"

"We are in real-time love now, there's no reversion to being-in-love. But I have to confess something. I think I am in love with the Marcus in love with being-in-love. You are in love with the Sandra in love with being-in-love, but we're past that now, to the real-life love, and no attempt to preserve the being-in-love will succeed. That being the case, I had better fetch my Garfield mug and Stirling Castle pencil."

"I was in love with being-in-love with you, Sandra."

"And I was in love with being-in-love with you, Marcus."

"Goodbye."

"I need to pack still."

3

H E MOURNED Sandra Acer's expired interest in him for two months before returning to his true love: reading. Forced labour is the nemesis of a power-reader, and Marcus had no desire to capitulate to capitalism. He devised a means to sate his literature needs without working while remaining in food and shelter: if he suffered the pain of labour for three years, surviving on a diet of frozen foods and lime cordial, remaining indoors and reading in bed with his bedside lamp the lone light burning in the flat, he would save enough to purchase a small cottage on the Isle of Orkney and, living a similar ascetic existence, he would read all the novels in the *1001 Books You Must Read Before You Die* list, compiled and edited by Dr. Peter Boxall. Once complete, he would surrender himself to the world of career and finance and crashing on the sofa watching the ninetieth episode of the latest must-see TV drama and spending his cash on overpriced ciders in faux-hip bars and impressing women and raising babies and whatever else he was supposed to do that didn't involve his true purpose.

That time had come. He located a cottage in Orkney known as "taigh-leughaidh," or the "reading-house." It was sold on the cheap: Clan McAllan had frittered their two centuries of crofting triumph at the roulette tables and flit to the mainland to find work in pizza restaurants. The latest budget crunch had cleared Scottish islands of their indigenous populations, leaving properties free for the salaried southerners to snap up as second homes. Marcus's needs were simple: a plug for his lamp, a reading chair, and a bookcase (in addition to a working fridge, shower, cooker, and a double bed and other amenities).

He had chosen the *1001 Books* compilation upon reading a favourable review on the website *The Bookwow Express*. Popular user Paul de Manné wrote: *This is the best millenary-plus-one of books available. (And not because I have a piece in there!).* A *millenary* of books. To scale the Ben Nevis of bookage: to crawl up the mountainface of literature,

6

crampons keeping one safe as one slipped up *Ulysses*, as one battled the unwelcoming conditions of The Rabbit Books, as one lost footing on *Giles Goat-Boy*, as one lost hope slushing through *The Poisonwood Bible*. Once complete, the nagging need to read all the time, the fear that one might reach 75 and never have read more than one's weight in novels, the preference for reading over interacting with friends and spouses, and the subsequent violent dissipation of those relationships, might vanish. Leaving him free to please whatever woman replaced Sandra Acer and attempt to fall in love with a non-text-based person.

The process of acquiring these 1001 books proved complicated. He had broken down his budget thus:

Annual Budget

Food	£960
Electric	£600
Tax	£1400
Books	£3500
Petrol	£100
Disaster Fund	£400

The sum of £3500 on books was an approximation. If each book was acquirable at 1p on Amazon marketplace, with additional postage costs of £2.80, this would cost him £2812.81 in total. However, while a large portion of the classics and well-known novels were available for that price, this failed to factor into account the lesser-known choices, or novels published overseas, or novels that were out of print on the list, or those in expensive print-on-demand editions. For these particulars, he included a margin of £700. He had searched the online catalogue at Kirkwall library, and found that 91 novels from the list were available to borrow, saving him almost 10% of the overall cost. For the novels on the list he had already completed, he substituted this for another work by the same author, and before he left, he made sure he had 20 of the novels with him to see him through the first fortnight.

On Writing
Origins of This

EXCUSE ME! I must . . . *make room, sir!* . . . impose myself . . . *oops, pardon madam!* . . . between these two . . . *squeeeeeze!* . . . chapters. There we are. That wasn't too painful. So, let's have a little breather. *Huuuuhhh.* (In.) *Hooooooooo.* (Out). Once more: *Huuuuhhh.* (In.) *Hooooooooo.* (Out). That's better. That is the problem with these novel things. Never a moment to stop and breathe. Between following this character's motivations and that character's intentions, having to keep up with conniving plotlines and overarching themes, *and* take the time to appreciate the workmanship and calibre of the writer's prose . . . so demanding! The reader has no choice, at times, but to place the book to one side and exhale. Nowhere in the text can she keep reading and have a metaphorical kick-back to absorb and ponder the proceedings. Look upon these interruptions (this is the first of an increasing number, unfortunately) as a place to kick-back and absorb (not that this novel is stressful on the level of complex character or plot—more on the level of relentless comedic pummelling), but also a place for me (the author) to share a few truths.

So, in the summer of 2016, I submitted to the Highland Council an application for their new First Novel Scheme, the first prize a £10,000 award to allow the winning writer to work on their novel set in the Highlands. The novel I intended to write was *A Tree Grows in Orkney*, a moving tale of recovery from alcohol addiction, finding new love after bitter divorce, and converting to Catholicism after a life of misanthropic atheism, featuring a character named Ben to whom those things happen. He opens an organic coffee shop in Kirkwall and marries a local pharmacist and embraces the forces of optimism. I never expected this trough of obvious feel-good swill to make it past the first selection process, but I had the bland avuncular hand of the bureaucrat helping me to the loot.

The selection panel consisted of two councillors (the first an avid reader of David Nicholls and Jojo Moyes, the second an avid reader of TV listings), one local poet with two published chapbooks (*Rain After the Rain*, Groundswell Press, 2009 and *Boat Atop the Boat*, Two Raptors, 2011), and two marketing people from the publisher (Acacia Tree Press) trained in targeting their middle-aged female readership with a master archer's pinpoint accuracy. I had written the pitch as a hoax (I had already published a novel earlier that year, the wartime satire *Fat Battlements*), and hadn't expected to receive a formal email congratulating me on the preliminary acceptance of my proposal from the ten thousand submitted for serious consideration of awarding me the prize money, based on a follow-up interview. I was "encouragingly invited" to meet the panellists the following week for an interrogation as to whether I was a worthy enough person to receive the award.

First, I had to cover my tracks. I had submitted the application from Edinburgh, having written the address of an uncle in Inverness to prove I lived in the Highlands. I took the five-hour morning bus to Inverness to meet the panel, with the intention of boarding the five-hour evening bus back upon being refused the cash. In an airless council office, the sort of place where mirthless civil servants cut the benefits of smack addicts and single mothers, I was welcomed and motioned to a chair before the five, who occupied a safe place behind an officious desk, the sort of positioning that told me: "We're nice and secure here, in our turrets of authority, whereas you, you smug scribbler, are some shabby little upstart who has merely waltzed in here thinking he is entitled to scoop up a fortune, and before we even offer you a cup of lukewarm water, we will assess the shit out of you."

The panel made me sweat.

No water was offered.

The first to speak were the councillors: two simpering balding males who regarded me with the frightened indulgence common to all bureaucrats who consider writers or artists anarchists liable to utter profound sentences about the human condition one second, and hurl flaming faeces into their children's faces the next. These two would be held accountable during the inevitable public backlash against the award. Their task was to minimise the damage by ensuring the cash went towards producing a cultural artefact valuable to all readers in the Highland area by larding regional references and trivia into reheated tropes. Knowing the public's basic resentment of handing over a single penny of their hard-earned wages to writers or artists—a public who regard the arts as something to be practised at home for the creator's own amusement and for their works to be made available for free to the public without them having to part with their hard-earned wages (cash more well-spent on £20 pizzas and £50 selfie sticks)—the councillors rattled their nervous questions at me.

"Is the proposed work *heartwarming*?"

"Is there a positive message delivered in an accessible manner?"

Then the publisher's marketing folk entered the fray, a hipper male-female twosome at home speaking to writers as if they were of the same species, and made unpleasant sounds with their mouths with inflections at the end:

"Is there an acceptable quota of violence and/or sexual content, written in a non-gratuitous way, that might help the book appeal to younger female or male readers, while not alienating the core middle-aged demographic?"

"Is the style poetic and/or lyrical?"

"Is the novel poetic enough so the reader never stops and says: 'This isn't worth £10,000 of my money!'?"

"Is the protagonist strong and empowering and a role model for young and old alike?"

"Is the novel long enough to keep the reader's interest but not too long to make them bored, and long enough so the book looks an impressive size on the shelf and large enough so the word 'Orkney' can be printed in huge letters on the cover?"

"Is the novel going to 'challenge' something or present an issue in an 'original' way, so that critics might use those words in reviews?"

"Is there an eccentric character, a tragic handsome character, a sexy female character, a dysfunctional family, a grizzled detective, or a cute kid? These aspects might play well in any television or film adaptations."

"Are you going to use any technical or arcane or overly lengthy words?"

"Are you going to write the book in such a way that anyone browsing in a shop will instantly purchase it after scanning a few pages?"

"Are you planning to structure the plot in chronological order, or leap back and forth in a potentially confusing way?"

To these questions I answered, with supremely faked confidence, the only thing I could:

"Yes."

Throughout the interrogation the poet had remained silent until the last ten minutes of the allocated hour, when the former fishmonger and plasterer whose pure blue peepers stared into the room at the blank specimen of panic before him, the one comrade I had in the room who could save me from this pain, shuffled the paper he had been doodling on to ask me: "Have you read Virginia Woolf?"

I had peered into this 48-year-old man's cerulean soul as the interrogative effluent seeped into my aching brain, hoping he might be the one to save me from the brutish bureaucrapping that the two men and one woman were performing with panache on my future, an ordeal punctuated only by my seventeen rictus affirmatives, but when I responded in the negative (I had read parts of *To the Lighthouse*, but this being an artistic matter I didn't expect the suits to wince), I realised that the poet took this lack of awareness as a deficit in literary experience: Woolf being to this poet the pinnacle of poetic prose, citing three famous scenes as examples, and stating in his humble manner that I should read her at once and write a book clotted with humorless lyrical waffle, free indirect narration on the shoulders of a buttoned bore, and use more nature imagery than there was in fact nature (not his words).

"Yes!" one marketer affirmed. "There have to be a certain number of descriptions involving beautiful scenery, as this novel will be released to coincide with the summer period to boost tourism."

"We're no literary experts, in fact the last book I read was *Inferno* by Dan Brown—a fantastic pageturner, by the way—but we think that water and wind should be the central metaphors. For example, if something dramatic happens between the characters, there should be a strong wind outside, and you can describe how that wind whooshes across the landscape, taking in various stunning aspects of that landscape in a state of wind-swept whooshedness. And perhaps the water crashing against the rocks can represent emotional turmoil happening to the characters, and you can show that in a detailed description of the weather and its place above the scene of the water crashing against the rocks as a metaphor and so on. These are ideas, like I say, we're not experts. But you should write that."

Next came the sizing up of me as a media maven. I would have to appear at Highland events in random ill-lit libraries where retired headmasters and headmistresses would pretend to listen to the novel-writing advice I stole from famous writers until the time came for them to speak about their non-fiction accounts of their remarkable ancestors, and ask their questions about how best to procure an agent for their important works. Then I would make a fleeting appearance on a panel with five other Highland writers at the Edinburgh Book Festival, failing to contribute much over the loudmouth American writer of hilarious bonk-busters set among monied rentiers whom the undersexed menopausal audience would coo over and laugh at the loudest. I would also have to be a trained interviewee, offering amusing but uncontroversial answers for a middlebrow readership, and perhaps—

"You might consider a beard," the woman said.

"Yes. Bearded male authors like Ned Beauman have polled high on the likeability index."

"I will," I said.

4

THE TRIP northwards: a mist-mooded morning with a mood-misted Marcus at the wheel of a small hatchback; a stabbing regret at having left a warm flat with wi-fi and powerful shower nozzle for a hovel in the middle of nowhere; a sequence of roads packed with vehicles zigzagging across various lanes for seven hours; a sense of freedom fabricated in part through upbeat indie music on the ipod ranging from The Apples in Stereo to The Undertones; a worsening cramp in both buttocks thanks to the cheap re-upholstering of the front seat at Freddie's Fixers Garage; a sequence of pre-bought paninis and wraps eaten at the wheel, and the filling overspill mopped from the crotch and thighs with a hankie; a nagging fear that the choice, met with amused indulgence by his sister, mother, and father, reduced his standing in the sanity community, and that at future Christmas meals, the episode might be treated in the same wordless manner as Uncle Hugh's nervous breakdown; a frightening encounter on the road to Thurso involving a five-second micronap and an impatient JCB; a reversion to talk radio and the hour-long feud between an imam and an atheist that made him relieved to leave the world of rolling news and current affairs; a misanthrope's sense of excitement at leaving human interaction behind and forging a self-reliant existence, coupled with a misanthrope's fear of crippling loneliness and alienation; a fond remembrance of barrelling up the A8 with Sandra Acer in their first month to visit her lactose and politically intolerant cousins, including the brief pit stop for a-huggin' and a-kissin' and a-spoonin'; an unprompted erection between Aviemore and Inverness; a persistent itch migrating from the left shoulder to the left nipple to the right hip to the right knee to the left ankle to the left heel and back again; an ominous cloud refusing to part with a drop; an attempted nap on the Thurso to Kirkwall ferry, interrupted nine times by two preteens debating the rad properties of Dizzie Rascal and Jay-Z; a fumble along the treeless landscape to locate the correct cottage; a second fumble across the treeless landscape to drive past the correct cottage; a third fumble across the treeless landscape towards the correct cottage; a sigh of resignation at the drear slab that was now home.

5

"Yes mum, I have arrived."

(After two hours spent driving past the place).

"Yes mum, the cottage interior is fine."

(The cottage interior had been spruced up with photoshop, showing little of the homeliness or warmth as seen in the pics. Callum Legdie refused all requests for a webcam viewing in favour of the pics taken in flattering sunlight and with the stains and cracks removed).

"Yes, the estate agent is reputable."

(The estate agent is a first-class huckster with wicked photoshop skills taking advantage of naïve desperates seduced by the nomadic lifestyle with a pre-mediaeval mistrust and hatred of mainlanders).

"Yes, the place is warm enough."

(If I manage to locate coal or firewood somewhere at this hour or locate seven twelve-bar heaters to plug into the damp sockets).

"Yes, there is a rustic vibe."

(If rustic vibe means the vibe of a passing spinster with no known relatives hoping to hasten her end by sitting unshawled before a dimming fire in a dust-laden room being spoon-fed by carers twice a day, and muttering hateful pronouncements against atoms).

"Yes, the previous owners cleaned the place."

(There isn't a rat infestation that I can see).

"Yes, I am comfortable . . . in the front room chilling on the sofa."

(Curled up in bed in arctic socks and a full suit and a beanie, with two hot water bottles).

"Yes, I will use the electric heater."

(If I want to be electrocuted).

"Yes, I have started reading."

(Once my fingers thaw).

"Yes, I will take care of myself."

(I will be dead by the morning).

"Bye."

(I am so cold).

6

H E WAS a voracious and shallow reader, perfectly content absorbing page after page of literary history, literary philosophy, literary literature, all and any things of a literary nature, allowing each fact and fancy to pirouette tantalisingly across his recall, only to topple backwards into the forgotten as the next fact arrived, his mind rapt and amazed and tingling at the point the words arrived, thereafter staggeringly incapable of recalling a kernel of the words read. He was an in-the-moment reader: savouring each sentence en route from eye to brain to oblivion, eating book after book until his head ached . . . and after a pop of paracetemol, he nosedived with delirium back into the text.

Over his morning oatmeal, wrapped in his winter coat in the living room, he began Flann O'Brien's *The Third Policeman*: a fabulous, philosophical comic novel combining the absurd freewheeling antics familiar to readers of O'Brien's *Irish Times* column, alongside innovative postmodern tricks presaging the future of that movement: its wholesale dismantling of the line between the real and the fictional. As he reached page 14, a light fixture from the ceiling came undone and landed four inches before his leather brogues, a sprinkling of dust coating his heels and toes. He nodded a nod that meant: "Yes, of course. Of course the dream I have nurtured for a lifetime, throughout those long hours on the phone with ill-bred halfwits accusing me of stealing their non-existent funds; the shouting matches with Sandra Acer when I lost faith in the power of words to bring two human beings together in harmony; the weekends steeped in cider and self-loathing, watching Al Pacino movies in a despairing loop; the endless battles with sleep and the page after a punishing nine hours on the phones, consuming coffee in copious slurps in futile attempts to remain awake; those carping voices telling me to kill the dream and that the novel is dead and the future is mindless work; the time lost, time lost, time lost, time lost, time lost, time lost, time lost, time never to be regained, lost, lost, lost, of course the light fixture will collapse, and the ceiling will come crashing down on top of me, and the rain and the wind will come to claim me before I even reach the fifteenth page. Of course, this dream will be a constant fight and a constant pain, causing me to doubt the dream in the first place, sending me back there, to that fucking nightmare I have tried to escape."

On Writing

More About This

H AVING NODDED along to their demands, I was presented with the "contract," where upon receipt of the first chapter, I would receive the first £5,000. The contract stated that I would deliver the novel "in the form discussed at the meeting." I signed and mooched around Inverness for four hours until the return bus unsped me home around midnight. I slept and the next morning wrote the first chapter. I included five detailed descriptions of prominent places of sublime comeliness and kept things safe by having Ben wavering over a bottle of vodka before collapsing in a sobbing heap in the arms of his redeemer and future wife, Alison. The contract permitted the panel to refuse the award if the first chapter was terrible, so I awaited the inevitable refusal email after I pinged the chapter to them after lunch.

Acceptance. The £5,000 was to be transferred tomorrow. I stared at the screen in disbelief and sought counsel from various friends and acquaintances.

Sister: "This is amazing! Write the book!"

Alex: "You're changing from an anti-writer's writer to a populist pap-pusher. Consider the impact writing this novel will have on your future reputation. People in the niche writing community will spit on your chin, and these people have a violent volume of sputum to spare. Niche publishers will tear up your novels and laugh hysterically in your face, citing that repugnant crowd-pleasing bestsmeller you wrote for money."

Tim: "Nom de plumeage. You know these lesser-known writers churn out bestsellers under fake names. James Patterson is FC2 board chair and novelist Lance Olsen. Stephen King is the riddle-writer and humorist Marvin Cohen. Paulo Coelho is the surreal comedic maverick Steve Katz. These so-called neglected writers are minted. Find a fake name, rake in the cash, and keep the anti-corporate cred."

Donna: "About time you earned some decent money, you reprobate. You owe society that novel, you disgrace."

Leonard: "Great idea! Heal those feelings of perpetual worthlessness at not earning a cent from your writing by writing a novel you will come to despise purely for the money you have made from it."

Fiona: "You know, you don't have to listen to their crap. Write an artistic masterpiece that stands on its own terms, and you will own those illiterate worms."

I chose Fiona's option. Having elected me that summer's Highland novel-writer, I held their knackers in a vise. I would write whatever I pleased and the panel of fussbudgets and Woolf-lovers would publish the results, and hire well-known authors to blow a Marlboro factory's worth of smoke up the novel's rear. At that time, I had ended a failing relationship with a female named Alice Rìos who had taken a post with Roget's Thesaurus. This provided her with an overspill of words with which to chide me for whatever transgression I had made that week—laziness, bookishness, va-va-voomlessness—all excuses for her reluctance to admit her defeat at having chosen me. Hoping the £10,000 award would reignite Alice's respect for me (first achieved when she read my writing, lost when she realised the writing was not worth vast sums), I chose to scram to Orkney to complete the deal.

I found a flat in Kirkwall and moved there with a suitcase and a laptop. Like Raymond Federman composing his seminal *Double or Nothing*, I aimed to hole myself up in the room surviving on microwave meals, and produce a masterpiece in record time. Alas, this was not to be the case. Enter: The Block.

A word for those writers who approach the blank screen with pepitude, revelling in the humble pleasure at creating worlds from words: bastards. I am the sort of artist who will spend weeks on end stood before the blank canvas, until one afternoon, I take a violent lunge and splatter the wall with colours, shapes, and blobs, then step back to ponder the carnage in despair, often tearing up the results and leaving the studio for months to hide. A week might have passed between the composition of this sentence and the last. (In fact, a month has passed).

7

To: callumledgie@highlandproperties.com
From: marcusschott@gmail.com

Dear Vampire,

You are a cancerous tumour on the Orkney-based property ladder. Your actions have resulted in the catastrophising of a planned utopia. I made the mistake of exposing my weakness to you. I made explicit my need for a sanctuary in the form of a cottage, and you consulted Ledgie's ledger, noticed a dismal drop in profits from last year, rubbed your claws together and thought: *Finalement, un imbécile je peux exploiter!*, only in English. I was promised a habitable environment with an acceptable quota of snugness. I have received a damp wilderness with an inacceptable quota of slugs' mess. You said the windows were double-glazed with glass. The windows are trouble-glazed with moss. You said the floorboards were solid enough to support a sumo wrestler. The floorboards are not solid enough to support a sumo tadpole. You said the ceiling beams could prop up a cathedral. The ceiling beams can't even prop up a catheter. You said the bed was the island of a thousand sleeps. The bed is the island of a million creaks. You said the toaster tanned one's bread to perfection. The toaster is still tanning bread from twelve hours ago. You said the cooker made succulent sausages and other meats. The cooker contains succulent sausages and other meats from previous owners. You see the pattern? In medieval China, there was a special torture for people like yourself. They would strap you to a rack, and flick you slowly with your Wallace & Gromit tie for months on end until your forehead collapsed. I will be blasting your sham outfit with a legal salvo soon.

Not Yours,

Marcus Schott-to-pieces

8

THERE WAS a problem with his order. The conglomerate bookstore said that the books he had ordered could not be shipped to his location without a surcharge of £10 per title. Marcus replied that the surcharge was a fucking ransom. The conglomerate employee replied that he was deeply sorry that these charges were necessary, only that the shipping to his location was complicated and a surcharge of £10 was required per book. Marcus replied that £10 per book was ludicrous as the books could be boxed together. The conglomerate employee replied that he was deeply sorry that the customer had been affected by these surcharges, and that if he wished to lodge a formal complaint, he could do so via this email address. Marcus replied that he would lodge a formal complaint if the outcome would be that the shipping surcharges were dropped. The conglomerate employee replied that he was deeply sorry, but they were unable to drop these surcharges as these are what was demanded to ship to his location. Marcus replied that one can't be deeply sorry three times, that one might have been deeply sorry the first time, but after the second and third sorries, that deepness would diminish, leaving behind a hollow sorriness, and next time he should say he was hollowly sorry. The conglomerate employee did not respond. Marcus lodged a formal complaint. Another conglomerate employee said he was deeply sorry, but there was nothing to be done about the surcharge, however, they were willing to refund the order and offer as a good will gesture, a £10 gift voucher. Marcus replied that if that £10 could cover the surcharge, and that his books could be boxed together, he would drop the complaint. The conglomerate employee replied he was deeply sorry, but the books were dispatched from different warehouses, so could not be boxed together, and a £10 would apply to each book, so that would total £220 for the 22 books he had ordered. Marcus replied HAHAHAHAHAHAHAHAHAHAHAHAHA-HAHA and requested the order be cancelled.

9

"HELLO, I would like a library card."

"Hello."

"Hello. I would like a library card."

"Yes. That shouldn't present a problem. One momentino please. I need to access the database which at the moment is bunged up with withdrawals."

"OK."

"Libros interruptus."

"What?"

"You are a new mug in these doors?"

"Marcus Schott from—"

"Save that name for the input stage! Be prepared for an accurate spelling on cue in under two minutes. I am Isobel Bartmel. I am a long-term server in this den of dust. Here we are . . . name please?"

"Marcus—"

"Spell."

"Em-eh-are-see-you-ess."

"Surname?"

"Ess-see-aitch-oh-tee-tee."

"Perfect. . . . No. Request invalid. Invalid. Invalid. It repeats itself in a red font. This is the blip to end all blips. KARRRRREEEEEN!! Excuse the horrible shouting. I need the bronchitic broad's expertise. Visiting here?"

"No. I have moved for a short while."

"It's always a short while. That's a syndrome known as Island Denial. I will tell you more. Are you free for a drink this evening?"

"I suppose so."

"Meet at The Swaddled Firkin at 7 pee-em?"

"Is that a pub?"

"Yes. Karen . . . fix this blip? This is Marcus Schott. He has moved here for a short while."

"A short while, eh?"

"Yes. A short while. I intend to inform him about Island Denial this evening when we meet at The Swaddled Firkin at 7 pee-em."

"Fixed. You two have fun."

"That was Karen. Despite her bronchitis she is able to resolve computational blips with the minimal of lip-aching small talk. That is the problem resolved. Your card should arrive within four to six weeks."

"Can I have something in the meantime?"

"No. Highland Council policies. No cardless visitors will have access to our priceless collections of Stephen King, V.C. Andrews, and Barbara Cartland until the authorised plastic rectangle is placed in their hands."

"I need books in a semi-urgent manner for something I am working on."

"Listen Marcus—I might be able to make an arrangement with you. More to come at The Swaddled Firkin."

On Writing

Alice Rìos

THIS IS not the sort of novel where the author reveals events from his life in intricate sleight-of-hand manoeuvres. No. This is the sort of novel where the author writes down what happened to him in matter-of-fact prose, tricking himself into believing the reader might find this approach refreshing in an era of pirouetting and eager-to-please writers who exaggerate each facet of their fascinating lives to trick themselves into believing their lives have "developed" in some significant way. This is the sort of novel where the author states what is happening at the time of writing. At present, I am in my study (yes, a study, although it isn't "mine" as I have and never will own property), writing this paragraph at 00.13 on a Saturday night while listening to *Medway Wheelers* by Billy Childish's noughties band The Buff Medways. Paragraphs like this, in their infuriating insignificance, contribute to the unfocused incoherence of the novel: a form in which I revel in the most (if unfocused incoherence might be considered a "form"—I think it can—or an anti-form, if you won't), for it asks nothing from the author except a consistent failure to pull things together in a satisfying manner, and forces the reader to strain hard to comprehend the author's non-existent intentions, and justify their own heroic effort to stagger toward the end of the novel, even if only to write a scathing online review of the novel. I hope that makes no sense.

To return to Kirkwall. I struggled with the novel. I walked along scenic cliff edges, seeking a single exploitable notion. I thought for the most part about the parting insults from Alice Rìos prior to our break-up. She told me that I was prone to boring prattle, that in fact, I had no intelligent conversation at all, and when she thought on our past, she failed to recall a single memorable utterance I had made in the whole time of our protracted union, and furthermore, the defence I used, that

I was more ordered in my writing, was laughable, because I made a point of avoiding coherence in my sentences, and in fact celebrated the sort of prattling non sequiturs I used in speech, meaning I would never complete a novel with a linear arc, or present a single idea with comprehensible logic. She also said I was so unmemorable in person that people who met me could neither remark that I was sullen nor uninteresting, for those who met me had no recollection of having met me at all, and that included people with whom I had interacted on a long-term basis, such as schoolfriends or colleagues or brothers. If I was incapable in sticking in a person's memory for less than half a second afterwards, and if I was incapable of producing one coherent sentence, I would never write a novel that would linger in someone's mind except as a vague memory of something that caused deeply unpleasant bafflement for over six hours. This is what Alice Rìos left me.

I still wanted Alice Rìos. I considered writing her a novel about a loser still in love with his ex who writes a novel to win back his ex. This was, from Alice's perspective, the worst idea. I needed to express a sincere emotion in a "proper" form: a sonnet, a linear narrative, a hallmark card. I was, of course, unable to express a sincere emotion unless I surrounded the true feeling in reams of rambling self-aware prose about being a hostage to the postmodern world where to express sentiments in the language of television was not a sincere form for me, and having this rambling self-aware prose itself provide the equivalent of the I-love-you, the I-am-so-sorry, without having to use those worn-out terms, except in scare quotes. For me, composing a postmodern novel about a writer composing a postmodern novel is a more sincere form of emotional expression than the I-love-you.

I opened a Word file entitled *A Sentimental Document*, in which I intended to commemorate everything I loved about Alice, committing the memories to paper before time swiped them, with the intention of sending this to her as a means of achieving what is sought in the nauseating idiom "closure." I was advised by Alice's mother this was a bad idea, partly to prevent me from sending a melodramatic screed of drivel and embarrassing myself, partly to uphold Alice's "no contact indefinitely" policy, meaning a response to such a document would never arrive, nor would the document probably be read in light of a final hysterical email sent as the last in a series of one-way correspondences. I mused on respectable literary ways in which I could use this emotionally upsetting experience in a manner that would also fulfil my sitcommercial desire for "closure"—a false form of restitution for unsatisfying events, required to help delude you into thinking one string-quartet-soundtracked moment might bring forth inner peace, when in life events merely trickle, fizzle, and peter out, and satisfying resolutions are in the end subbed in favour of hardcore forgetting. I would never, unless I chose to keep a private collection of written memories for repeated nostalgic torture upon their discovery (I am convinced all nostalgia is a form of self-torture, urging you to recall long-buried events and their miserable outcomes in a perpetual loop), commemorate the relationship with specific references to actual events, and loving signals to Alice, whose friendship I still desired at the end, and for whom my affection remained stubbornly undimmed, despite her rather bluntly forbidding communication, with only the promise of a friendly greeting should our paths ever cross again accidentally, and that to write such a work would be to preserve a still relatively recent point of view, meaning that at some point in the future, having had no contact for many years, my heart may have utterly hardened towards her, solidified somehow by the long forced exile, and that a potentially unread encomium of a person who spurned me may prove embarrassing at a later date. Leaving the only course of action to write nothing at all, or to write something like this.

10

To READ 1001 books over three years, an average of 334 books per year was required, meaning 6.18 books per week, 0.915 books per day. This meant the near-completion of one book per day, or in the case of longer books, the completion of one over a few days, balanced with several shorter ones on another day, not accounting for the one-week no-reading allowance he permitted himself. The moments not reading would be taken up with feeding himself, performing household repairs and chores, fetching foods and utilities, writing emails or conducting telephone calls with friends and enemies, taking the minimal exercise needed to last three years without perishing. The narrowest crevice had been permitted for socialising. The building and maintaining of friendships was too time-consuming, so the occasional pint and banter with a barman was all that would work in the timeframe. Time-intensive measures, such as meeting a librarian in a bar, needed to secure the right books, were crucial.

He drove to Kirkwall—a capital nestling under a constant cumulonimbic paranoia—and parked outside the unwelcoming hump of bricks known as The Swaddled Firkin. A parade of swizzles lined the bar, their monochrome consumers hunched over taking listless laps, hoping to absorb the colours into their ontologies and stagger into the streets with a newfound vibrance. Marcus scanned the standard 1970s pub décor for traces of Isobel. One man in a tweed blazer, fresh from a successful piss, walked past the cheerless Marcus and winked, fumbling for his zip below the untucked shirt, and returned to his bar stool to lap at the colours. A short corvine woman rotating her head in impatient expectation was nooked in a booth. This was Isobel.

"Hi Marcus. Sit on that seat," she said, pointing to the seat ahead. "I prewarmed it with the warmth from these stockinged feet," she said, pointing to her stockinged feet on the seat.

"That's some feat," Marcus said.

"Thanks. My mother once remarked that I have outbending toes. That isn't even a word. You said feat, F-E-A-T, not feet F-E-E-T. I see that now. I preordered a lemon swizzle, have a sip and pass comment."

"Mmm. Yes."

"These are a Kirkwall quirk. You observe the line of bachelors at the bar. A common complaint in this town is the absence of vibrance. Life under a leaden pall is not conducive to being fabulous. Men in their fifties onwards in particular suffer from this condition and medicate with kaleidoscopic cocktails."

"You can taste the purple."

"You can! Once in a while, some Angus Macneil stumbles onto Meadow Drive singing hits from *Grease*. I attribute this to the Purple Powwow's potent properties. P-p-p-pow!, as we often remark here."

"I taste Parma Violets."

"Parma Vio*lents*. And parma ham. Shaved thin."

"Tell me about the books."

"You mainlanders! No patience for our island flim-flam. First up: Island Denial. You see, when a mainlander moves here for a 'short period of time,' that opens a truth vein: his failure to succeed in a metropolis, his peevish retreat to an island to flipoff the world, and his false belief that he will return victorious. The truth is few 'short-term' residents ever leave. This island is not a dosshouse for mainland rejects. This is a demanding and unforgiving place, where survival is twice as terrible. You have two options here. You either become fabulous, like me, like some others, or retreat inward into self-hell. By fabulous, I mean become a kind of character, carve out a niche for yourself on the island. People will see you then. If you aren't seen here in a positive light by another human being . . . that's the end."

"The end?"

"Imagine living here and having no one except those drabs at the bar and barmen who vanish when the drinks are poured."

"Ah."

"There are bells along the bar so the barmen don't have to stand around waiting on the drunks."

"I came here to be alone, in fact. I came here to read. I want to complete the *1001 Books You Must Read Before You Die* list, edited by Dr. Peter Boxall."

"You came here to read a thousand books?"

"Yes. So I need access to the library."

"You've placed a puzzling notion lapwards. I might need to order a Mango Mangler to boost these brain cogs. Let me recap. You travelled up to this historic but anaesthetic island to rot in isolation reading some other bugger's favourite books?"

"Not one bugger. Multiple buggers."

"Sheesh. Those is some potent motive. I suppose I can sling a few books towards that bemusing Marcus head for the purpose of reading."

"Thanks."

At that point the conversation dried up, Isobel stunned at such wanton literateness, and the textual maw into which Marcus was fated to fall, and at the explicit semaphore one of the swizzler swiggers was making towards the barmaid, whose milk-white visage made her a target for their stoppered cocks.

II

HIS WEEKEND: a frustrated attempt to read *Borstal Boy* over the shrieking of the kitchen pipes; an awkward phone call from Callum Ledgie regarding the "slanderous" nature of his "vilely literary" email; the first attempt to toast a slice of white bread in the one functioning appliance; the realisation that no hot water was to emerge from the bath or shower taps; the fast surge of intense pain and rage at the unfairness of the universe, and the promise whispered into a cracked wall tile that Callum Ledgie would find himself strangled in his bed come sundown; a second attempt to read *Borstal Boy* over the collapse of an apse; a severe pacing up and down of the various rooms as pounds and pence somersaulted before him, perfoming a dance à la *Día de los Muertos*; the ongoing battle to turn the toast to a semblance of crispness after twelve minutes; the overwhelming desire for a Punitive Pineapple swizzle; the lapse into dreams of sitting before a roaring fire finishing up his 1001st novel with a satisfied sigh; the cold reality of the cracks he had made in the floorboards pacing up and down; a fifteen-minute sulk on the sofa wrapped up in his winter coat; the last futile attempt to read *Borstal Boy* over the moan of "help me" coming from the cottage's cavities; a furious retreat to his car to locate and punch Callum Ledgie; an enraged drive to the Highland Properties office in Kirkwall, including the near-flattening of a rodent and two close swerves into ditches; the arrival at the Highland Properties where a man sat behind a desk clicking a mouse with a neutral expression.

12

"ARE YOU the verminous worm known as Callummox Ledger?"
"Mr. Schott, I presume."

"This is the place where dreams are soused in kerosene and set alight."

"Please take a seat."

"This is the place where the seeds of imagination are riddled with cankers."

"You are not pleased with the cottage?"

"This is the place where hope is shot in the face with a pistol."

"You appear to view me as some metaphorical representation of the brutal triumph of commerce over art. Of course, as an estate agent, I have no interest in art or the imagination, however, I can understand the impulse others have to validate their lives through the creation of works over the making of monies. I am alone here, so I can't have Hector pour a free espresso into a mug for you. A water?"

"No. I want to poke around in that devious cellar of a mind. You sat in this office and faked those photos. You took the picture of a rotting basement and used Photoshop CS6 to remove the moss and mushrooms. You took the pestilential atmos of the kitchen and with the addition of sunlight transformed it into a catalogue paradise. You made a damp bathroom with cracked tiles look like the Queen's WC."

"Mr. Schott. Here's a fundamental of estate agenting: make the properties look appealing. I couldn't sell Clan McAllan cottage in its current state if I posted honest pictures. You see the obviousness?"

"I came up here to read 1001 books. I need warm rooms and hot water. Your ruin has neither of these things."

"I read one of those 'novels' once. It was about a man who ate a squirrel. The most bizarre thing. The man captured the squirrel, named him Arnold, then slow-roasted him in the oven for three weeks. He served the squirrel to his friends with tartare sauce around a dinner table, where the topic of abortion was discussed for nine hours, no one commenting on the squirrel being forked into their mouths. I decided on the basis of that experience never to read a 'novel' again. I assume they are all like that."

"Will you repair the cottage?"

"That wouldn't be wise. Incur an enormous bill of over £100,000 fixing a sold cottage?"

"I will hurt you."

"I should make you aware, Mr. Schott, of my father's involvement in the Orcadian crime syndicate known as The Bolt. My father, Lennox Ledgie, operates a peaceful yet violent union of insane yet kindly psychopaths, whose sole purpose is to utterly fuck up, with good grace, anyone who crosses him. I am the son, therefore crossing me is crossing Lennox. That is the thing of which you should be aware."

On Writing

Creative Guidance

I RETURNED TO the task of writing a masterpiece that might convince the council to keep sending me money, beginning with the scene where Marcus leaves his tedious office with a flourish. I sent this opening chapter to the councillors after several threatening emails demanding some evidence of movement in their investment. It soon became apparent from the emails that this was not pleasing to them.

Councillor #1

I have read the opening chapter, and I have to say, I have a few reservations. First, this is not the opening chapter from the original submission. I was not expecting such a radical change in direction. Your first paragraph is a block of speech from the main character to someone on the phone announcing his resignation in a bizarre manner. I am no literary critic, but I have to say, no one alive talks like this. The character says: "allow me to insert a fact-filled eclair into that whining piehole [sic] of yours," a ridiculous line, completely unlike normal human speech. It is more probable that character would say "let me tell you something" or "shut up, I have something to say." To help you along, I have rewritten that opening for you in a manner I think more accurate to everyday speech:

"Mrs. MacDonald. My name is Marcus. Listen to me for a second. This is my last day on the job, so I feel I can be more candid with you than I might be usually with callers. By signing up for a loan with us, you may find yourself in the long run in a less stable financial position than if you went elsewhere. I wouldn't normally do this, but I would completely avoid our company, which is disreputable at best. Regards."

I hope this is useful. I suggest using this is a springboard and building the story from there.

Best,

Councillor #1

Thank you for your opening chapter. Although this new opener is somewhat amusing, I would recommend returning to the material submitted previously.

Yours,

Councillor #2

Marketers

We have read the opening section and have some comments. First, having two whole names in the opening sentence is confusing for readers. The reader will panic at having to memorise two character names in such a short space, put the book down at once and reach for one with no or one character name. Next, the contrast of "eclair" with "piehole" will upset readers: to combine sweet with savoury like this will leave a bad taste in their mouths. Next, the words "cessation" and "interdepartmental" are too large too soon. Readers will find that pretentious and dismiss the author as an indulgent elitist. Next, the trivia and references. The factoid about Neptune is forcing contemplation too soon, straight after the reader is struggling to remember the names, and those foreign street names are intolerable. Next, the satirical remarks about the loan company, while amusing, are somewhat incendiary too soon. Later in the novel, if you want to make a remark about the inner workings of a Kafkaesque (there's a word you could use!) office, that would be acceptable. We can't figure out what market you are targeting in this opener. This sort of thing would never find a wide, or even niche, audience. Even if you're shooting for an audience who like offbeat and strange fiction, this sort of opening is too indulgent, there are few people who will tolerate this sort of thing.

Best

Marketers

13

MARCUS TRAVERSED the unwooded plateau contemplating the various flavours of denial. The first—classic vanilla—involved nurturing the pretence that things might turn out fine in spite of the insurmountable obstacles, and that some intervention or eureka solution might present itself at the last minute. The second—cookies and cream—involved the nurturing of a new pastime to replace the old one, such as repairing the cottage, in the hope that the original ambition might be resumed at a later date. The final—raspberry swirl—involved the acceptance that the whole plan was in tatters, all that scrimping and saving ruined through the rogue actions of Callum Ledgie and his mafioso cronies, and that copious beers and vodkas might somehow reignite the hope that had been snuffed in his heart.

Upon his return, Isobel Bartmel was stood at the cottage door in a pair of polkadotted leggings and a snooker professional's waistcoat. At her feet were sixteen novels in four stacks of four. Her small face, her bonny boniness, her stretched smile lines, her fat forehead and thin fringe, hove into view as Marcus hopscotched up the remaining paving slabs, and formed an expression of surprise: from her behaviour at The Swaddled Firkin last night he wasn't surprised to see her (she had riffed for three hours on the library's clientele, and her unexaggerated role in each of their lives). She spoke first on her fondness for snooker—her parents had a table outside their mobile home, on which she sunk pinks and potted blacks within their Sunday afternoon bonding window—and explained that she found the waistcoat snug around her scrawn. Next she spoke about the essence of the Orcadian *remote*: each cottage along the sprawling coast was separated by two miles of verdancy, spaces that closed one's mind to the realm of thought and were intended to keep residents hooked on the hollow spectacle of such open loveliness in contrast to the spaceless huddle of a metropolis.

American Psycho was visible on the first pile. She spoke on Hannah Arendt's famous banality of evil notion in relation to Bateman's passionless slaughtering to the music of Genesis, and how local serial killer Thorfin Dramp's 2012 murders had been committed to a soundtrack of Coldplay, Adele, and Keane. *Claudine's House* was visible in the second pile. She spoke on how Colette's brutal husband had forced her to pen a series of novels to be published under his name, and the dopiness of publishing four novels about a little girl's upbringing and education from a feminine perspective under the name "Willy." *Morvern Callar* was visible on the third pile. She spoke of the aimless protagonist's opportunism and our need to leap at any chance we have of escaping our own monotony. *Keep the Aspidistra Flying* was visible on the fourth pile. She spoke on the sexiness of following one's ambitions, and how Gordon Comstock's hopeless verse, scribbled in his damp room, was worth more in life than a million balance sheets showing zillions in profits, and that she had fantasised about being Rosemary Waterlow, and being taken by Gordon in the long grass.

Marcus, caught up in the pleasing whirl of her discourse, invited her inside.

14

"I AM NOT being sarkus Marcus, but this place is a lump of ouch," she said. He realised there were no cups, no coffee, no functioning kettle, and no hot water, and an inferno of shame raged on his face.

"I was shafted. Callum Ledgie. He is the member of The Bolt."

"Yes. A fine bowling team."

"Pardon?"

"The Bolt is the name of the estate agents' bowling team."

"Noted."

"Listen. Sit on this sofa. Let me use words to explain this. I came because this 1001 Books scheme is oblate. You are taking on this world in the wrong plimsolls. I offered old Frank Horse a similar oral. He was planning to read the complete back issues of *The New Yorker* to expire in a cocoon of wit and sophistication. He was kidding himself. The sharp Harvard-strength *bon mots* would sail past Frank's head. You have come here to read the sort of novels that need a beating heart to be appreciated. You can't read novels that reflect the warp and woof of life in this crumbling hole. Your blackened soul will render the words enemies: soon pure hatred will overwhelm the oculars. You will read nothing. You will sit in a casserole of abhorrence and expire in a mush of carrots and brisket."

"Thanks for the advice. But I have to do this. I was put on this planet to read words on pulp."

"At least come to mine. I have chicken drumsticks, mineral water, and central heating."

"I couldn't impose."

"I also have a working shower."

"Let's go."

Isobel occupied a cottage on Willowburn Road. Once inside, she produced a plate with chicken drumsticks and invited Marcus to munch. Her interior reflected the unpindownable "character" she had made for herself on the island—a poster of snooker champion Ronnie O'Sullivan sat next to a canvas print of Picasso's *Woman with Mustard Pot* and a framed picture of The Wedding Present's *Seamonsters*. Her bookcase also reflected this willed eclecticism: biographies of Margaret Thatcher, Gandhi, Tony Benn, and Tony Blair, her fiction ranging from William H. Gass's *The Tunnel* to Jacqueline Wilson's *The Bed and Breakfast Star* to Paulo Coelho's *The Zahir*. One thing Marcus had been unable to trap in his short life was the logic behind women's bookshelves. Sandra Acer would spend hours defending her right to read and keep on her shelves the insipid crime procedurals of Quentin Jardine, and proceed to read several in between the works of Gertrude Stein, Virginia Woolf and Marguerite Duras. Other women in his life had shelves featuring Barbara Taylor Bradford beside Kurt Vonnegut, Chris Moyles beside David Foster Wallace, and Harper Lee beside Paul Ableman. Isobel, at least, was open about her intention to baffle.

She took him upstairs to show him her collection of vintage bottle tops and newspaper clippings of flood warnings. She closed the bedroom door and removed her waistcoat, her tank top, her skirt, and polka-dotted leggings. She stood upright at the door in her triangular pants, her petite bra like a blindfold across her petite breasts. Marcus assessed her two long twigs, the navel in its flat stomach, the auburn hair running down her wiry shoulders and, unable to burst into desire, focused on stammering incredulity. "What are you doing?" he asked. Isobel, her head bowed in a coy vigil, allowing Marcus another chance to assess her semi-nude form and will himself into arousal, approached from the door. "You remind me of Gordon Comstock," she said. As her blank face neared his bland face, he stared at her bow-like lips, thought "lips, lips, lips" and "woman, woman, woman," and with more encouragement from his ardour, willed himself into passion with repeated violent kissing. "Call me Rosemary," Isobel said when removing Marcus's unclean clothing. Marcus nodded assent, intending to do no such thing and hoping for a swift and painless penetration. Fortunately, with Isobel's Orwell-inspired ardour, this happened to their mutual satisfaction.

15

THINGS HAPPENED to Marcus of a not unpleasant nature. He had paused in mid-dangle over the void, and with Isobel's assistance was beginning his slow prod back to stability, what she called his "rehabthrillitation." He sprawled on her sofa reading Iain Banks's overrated and tedious first novel on hymenopteran torture while she fetched and returned and stamped trash for bored widows and cash-strapped tourists waiting for their ferries. He drained a pint of cola, slurped a bowl of minestrone, and read Janice Galloway's intense étude on mental illness *The Trick is to Keep Breathing* while she inhaled last year's dust and spoke about the increasing density of Mrs. Gambol's scones at the church fête with her co-workers. Following Isobel's seduction, Marcus traded on his Comstockian appeal—the sole reason for the romping and rescue—and spoke about his contempt for capitalism and the escape through literature he had devised. Her ears honied to the sound of these defiant ideals and further sexual intercourse followed, some of which Marcus found pleasurable.

"You might consider this Orwell sex fetish I have in poor taste," Isobel said one afternoon after work while removing her coat and placing her keys on the table and nuking a Yakult from the fridge. "But I have always found George's depiction of sex and love thrilling in its doom. You see, Gordon is unable to surrender to passion because of Rosemary's fear of expensive babies. She refuses penetration in the grass, and later, capitulates to Gordon's lust with a depressing shag in his damp room. As Gordon is slowly bending before the Money-God, Rosemary sacrifices her practical nature to please him with this depressing forced hump. But their coupling is misaligned. And in *1984*, the liberated Julia lures Winston to her bed with an unbelievable love note passed in the corridor. That Orwell fails to convince us of this couple's love outside the symbolic device makes the lovers' plight twice as painful. I suppose what I attempt in these sexual encounters is to fuck the love into Orwell. You know George was a keen reader of Henry Miller's *Tropic of Cancer*? Boggles the brain."

"You are sleeping with me to fuck the love into a fixed fiction?"

"No. You are an interesting manlette. I use the suffix -lette since I see oodles of child in Marcus. The last male I had sexual relations with was rather Winstonesque in his naïve yearning for the release of pain in the arms of a vibrant sexual being. That being being me. Once he'd kicked his PCP habit I was tossed aside and replaced with a D-cupped ditz from Thurso."

"Sorry."

"S'ok. I understand the need to pass into the page. We are all wandering around this squalid planet with our little brains failing to fire at the right moment and our feet leading us into quarries filled with armed lunatics; running from barroom to courtroom with no shitting clue what led us to hack up a sailor's pet rabbit with a machete, or torch an orphanage after watching *It's a Wonderful Life*; and through these books, these beautiful books, we can create an alternative world in our heads, populated with the sort of vivacious rapscallions and fantastic fellows we'd never encounter at the bus stop, and make a home, plant a fucking flag, and live there, on our own private moon, floating forever above the earth, freeing ourselves from the stifling agony of having to fight to live in another fucker's system."

"My Lord."

"Sorry, I am sermonising. Spooning sugar into those lugs. This is part of your rehabthrillitation. Or should I say, your rehabthrillititillation?" She removed her clothes and began licking Marcus's knees.

"That's some coinage," he said.

"If this were a novel," she said, "there'd follow some fumbling attempt to render this fuck in word form."

The sex act: Isobel's feverish knee and leg lickings, her tongue lapping at his hairs like a parched calico cleaning the milk-bowl; Marcus's tolerance of this peculiar technique and hope that she might rise towards the penis and administer lappings of an equally vicious nature;

Isobel's passing over the penis and launching her light frame onto Marcus's belly, shooting her tongue into his open mouth and serving up a series of succulent kisses punctuated with loud "mmm" sounds to emphasise the intense smack of these lip attacks; Marcus's instant erection upon impact of these lip-smacking kisses, followed by a mad lunge to squeeze flesh in all its forms, starting with hard tugs on her upper shoulders, a fast descent down her back, arriving at two careless squeezes of her buttocks; Isobel's swift insertion of Marcus's penis into her vagina and the beginning of the rutting proper; Marcus's mad lickings of her erect nipples, his feeling that these nipples were the finest thing in the universe, and the intense pleasure upon each pinch and lick and suck; Isobel's imagining herself as Rosemary being fucked by Gordon in the grass after twice refusing him, conceding to his pleadings as his hard member bangs against her clenched thighs, trying to force itself into her wet area, and the thrill of opening her legs to him and soothing his pain; Marcus's picturing Sandra Acer's ample tits and plump buttocks, and his time sucking and lapping at them both like a lunatic; their mutual sense of impending eruption, and their mutual eruption with drool spilling out their mouths, seminal fluid shooting up Isobel's tubes, and Isobel's fluids oozing on his legs, and the blissful collapse back on the sheets once the whole sordid spectacle was finally complete.

"I'm glad this isn't a novel. A description of that would be absolutely revolting," Marcus said after.

On Writing

An Aigeann

AS PART of the contract, I was required to lead various workshops at the Rousay retreat, *An Aigeann*. Like most of the tutors, I had no prior knowledge of teaching and arrived armed with a dozen printouts of Hallmark card advice from famous writers, tried-and-tested useless wisdom parroted down the ages by millions of clueless pedagogues. The attendees had self-financed their stays at the retreat, putting extra pressure on me to make profound sounds and offer useful feedback on their works. I decided the easiest method of survival was to offer patronising praise on their individual works, and to send them home humming with misguided self-belief to continue making the same mistakes in their sentences: at least this would stop the talented ones from flourishing for a little longer.

The workshop attendees were, for the most part, retirees seeking praise on their wartime memories and pedantic genealogical hagiographies, alongside a few student poets and one or two serious-looking normals, who I would have to work extra hard to flatter. One of these was Flora Fauna, whose "novel was being optioned" at that time, whether for publication or an intern to read the first ten pages, she didn't explain. She hit me with some precise questions about her prose— "Do the instances of antonomasia disrupt the sentence's staccato bounce?" "Are these clauses creaking under an anastrophic heft?"—to test whether I knew what those terms meant and out me as an impostor. Fortunately, I could fathom their meanings from a read of the evident clumsiness in the chosen sentences. "Yes, I would recommend topiarising the latter and stripmining the former," I replied, hoofing terminology. She responded with an unconvinced smirk that signalled later there would be a second and third and fourth round and I would be exposed in her eyes as a hoofy blagger.

I taught a class on style, using that old favourite, the opening of *Lolita*, to show how writing that far exceeded the abilities of everyone present could be imitated and copied to bring their own writing up to a level of acceptable imitation to enable it for consideration for the Booker or Orange Fiction Prizes. The retirees interrupted me several times as I praised the alliterative bounce (wink to Flora) of Vlad's opener to complain that this was irrelevant to their works, and ask when were they going to get the chance to read their work aloud. A few weeks later, I had to endure Bill McAlpine reading his ungrammatical account of his father, a mechanic who changed wheel nuts for the entirety of the Second World War, taking long pauses after moments he considered impressive, waiting for the audience to make some appreciative noise, which they did to make him hurry up in the form of a mild "ooh." Mhairi Post followed, with her Grandfather the Respected Lawyer, narrating with hauteur her important Grandfather's bog-standard lawyering activities, also seeking and receiving mild "ooh"s. Flora had vanished for a toilet break two seconds into Bill's reading and never returned.

I praised the memoirs. The retirees believed that their personal histories were liable for consideration at large publishers, and would send copies to every single non-fiction venue in the Yearbook. I told them that personal histories were of no interest to publishers, except in the case of exceptional or famous people, and with affronted faces, they replied that their relatives *were* exceptional, thank you. After several years of pointless email and letter exchanges, and in some cases, stalking agents at literary festivals, they would self-publish their books featuring cover art of a random field in monochrome, or sepia-tinted old photos of dead people as young people, and move on with their lives.

16

To: callumledgie@highlandproperties.com
From: marcusschott@gmail.com

Dear Liar,

It has come to my attention that "The Bolt" is not the name of an Orcadian crime syndicate but the name of a bowling team. This means "liar" is the apt appellation for you, Mr. Ledgievil. You hoaxed me with the threat of murderous lunatics to avoid having to cope with the inconvenience of dealing with one of your dupes. Let me tell you something. I am a violent and unstable man. You have thrown my *raison d'être* to a pack of starving wolves. I am in contact with my legal help Sue U. Hard and what she refers to as her "evisceration of lawyers." She specialises in cutting apart little men and serving them cold on a bed of tarragon and rice. Another thing: "The Bolt" is a stupid name for a bowling team. To bolt means to run fast. Running fast has nothing to do with bowling. In fact, apart from the several spasms involved in throwing the ball, bowling is one of the most sedentary pastimes available. Perhaps someone thought "bolting" is what happens to the ball on its trip towards the skittles. This is "rolling." The team should be called "The Roll" or some variation on that verb. I am also proficient in the locking and loading of a howitzer. I specialise in crosshairing crass, hairless twerps who cheat well-intentioned men with a full head of hair out of their expensive cottages. You see?

Never yours,

Marcus Great-Schott

17

OVER A Fructose Fusillade swizzle at The Swaddled Firkin, Marcus entered the parsimonious realm of Gordon Comstock. At the bar, characterless islanders swallowed tankards of colour and sat hunched in their sad kaleidoscopes. One man, hooked on Avocado Ackack, had an elm-green complexion, and was refused a fifth pint by the unsympathetic barman, who felled him out on the pavement. Orwell's novel is a trenchant exploration of the artist's dilemma—to chose food and the familiar over starvation and the making of art—written in his customarily blunt and pellucid prose style. From across the room, a tall man with a cerise luminescence on his cheeks interrupted Marcus on page nine.

"Reading socialist miserablism on this sunny day?" he said. The rain shat sheets outside. Marcus, taking control of his head in the nanosecond between its automatic tilting upwards to see the face that made those words, mused on whether to force the speaker into making more words to declare his presence, and at the same time crib cred for seeming so involved in the novel as to have blocked out the world, or to raise his head at once and attempt a similarly literate remark in spite of his head being stuffed with this stuff.

"Yes . . . Orwell," was the awful response.

"Orwell or Wells? *Qui est le meilleur?*" the man asked. He had taken a seat opposite Marcus and placed his Tomato Tankage on a beermat. "Herbert was a hack with Big Ideas, Eric was a hack with Big Ideals. Herbert takes his working class heroes to the top and back again. Eric takes his working class heroes to the sewer then the cesspool."

"Yes. I'm Marcus," he said.

"I am Raine Upright," the man said. "I trust you are familiar with Orwell's magnum opus, *A Clergyman's Daughter*? You see, numbskulls overlook this for its flirtation with the experimental, and even Orwell himself called the novel 'bollocks.' The fact is this work showcases Orwell the artist. Inspired by the Wandering Rocks and Circe chapters of *Ulysses*, Orwell set about crafting a novel that pushed *form* not content. Alas, the label of artist was not a comfortable one for pragmatic Eric, and a hack he remained."

"Are you from here?"

"I occupy Clan McLannan cottage."

"I am here to read 1001 books."

"I hope there's no middlebrow shit on your list. You know, pastel covers with acacia trees. I have a vast set of bookshelves at the cottage. Let's head back there and sink some of the cheap Australian swizzle from the fridge."

Proceeding from The Swaddled Firkin along the historic streets past the historic cathedrals and their historic architraves, the two arrived at Clan McLannan cottage, an historic building owned by an historic family, who hysterically fled to the mainland in an historical fit of histrionics upon learning Hispanics with histamines had moved into an historic house next door. Raine explained that he was a former lecturer at Thurso Polytechnic, and had been thrown out for ranting against the syllabus, forcing students to read his own favourite texts, among them the out-of-print four-book utopian sequence *The Daily Lives in Nghsi-Altai* by Robert Nichols, and the entirety of Robert Burton's *The Anatomy of Melancholy*.

"You see, the box-licking halfwits wanted me to push *Emma* and *Frankenstein* on these texting cherubs. You could see the boredom in their emoji-ridden eyes, the weariness at having The Canon fired at them. A canon exists to be defied. The reading list I offered was a provocation: make your own canon, I was telling them. No one needs, at the sexually volcanic age of seventeen, to have Austen and her prim obsession with marrying off bland ladies to men of the right social class. At that age, I was sexually ravenous, all I read were the novels of Miller, Roth, and Updike. Colleges and universities refuse to acknowledge that all their pupils want to do is to hump repeatedly, rapturously, and rebelliously, until the novelty wears off and their intellects can evolve free from the constant throb of Eros. You can't write up a syllabus of lechery, of course, without an investigation. In fact, you can't even mention fucking in front of students without an investigation. To a seventeen year old, the teacher is a sexless pusher of intelligence over sensuality, and sex is the domain of the young and randy, and everyone over twenty having sex is a revolting creep. I was once hauled into the Manager's office for placing *Tropic of Cancer* on the reading list. I explained to the bean counter that Orwell himself, even, for all his moth-eaten blazered impotence, found the sexual avarice of Miller an important and liberating thing. Love or loathe Miller's egocentric rutfests, the man *napalmed* the sex taboo in literature. If that doesn't deserve a place on the syllabus over *The Castle of Otranto*, my name is Rick Astley."

"I am reading the 1001 texts on Dr. Peter Boxall's list."

"Ooofffttt! That fraud? Fuck reading that prescribed arseclamp. The same old same-olds. I edit a periodical called *Up Yer Syllabus*, released monthly, containing the antidote to the sort of ill-read herdism Boxass and co promote. I am talking the crème of the under-read. The stuff flattened under fat fashionista arses, forgotten in the waft of mainstream farts. Here's a sample issue. Have a read. Now let's sup these 2013 Aussie Durifs."

18

THERE FOLLOWED a plonk-driven exchange of muddled ideas, including Marcus's theorem that reading shite fiction might help improve one's skills and motivate one as a writer; Raine's opinion that the more senile Nabokov became, the more readable his novels, citing *Look at the Harlequins!* as an example of the Master loosening up his preciously hewn style; Marcus's belief that estate agents were the epitome of the cash-sucking capitalist mentality that was forcing literature towards the precipice of culture; Raine's opinion that Nicole Krauss's *The History of Love* was winner of The Most Boak-Inducing Title Contest, and that novels with those sorts of names were predestined to send the blubbering female masses into frenzies of tears and compassion and win the fuck out of awards; Marcus's fear that no amount of reading was likely to save him from the ever-widening chasm that was his soul, and that literature was nothing more than a pleasant means to pass the time before the grave; Raine's opinion that encyclopaedic novels brought more pleasure than climbing mountains or leaping from planes, and that those thrillseeking arseholes who strap themselves into parachutes for kicks should pick up a copy of *Laura Warholic*, *Three Trapped Tigers*, or *Infinite Jest*; Marcus's concern that Callum Ledgie had phoned the police following his unsubtle email threat, and that if so, he could phone the police too following Ledgie's verbal threat about "The Bolt"; Raine's opinion that the works of Will Self constituted the finest body of comedic and satirical writing in Britain of the last twenty-five years; Marcus's opinion that a stain on the cottage wall had metamorphosed into The Fat Controller, and was about to run them over in his steam train; Raine's rebuttal that the stain was in fact Septimus from Rikki Ducornet's *Entering Fire* on the rampage with a soldering iron; Marcus's belief that Raine's take on literature was too elitist; Raine's enraged reply that Marcus was a fucking middlebrow shitmuncher, munching down the middlebrow shit and begging for more; Marcus's defensive response that Raine should chill the fuck out and snack on a little Khaled Hosseini; Raine's rebuttal that *The Kite Runner* was sort of issuetastic fiction that turned up-to-date, politically loaded topical material into powerful works of stating the obvious, and whose sole purpose was to educate the Uninformed or Casually Interested Westerner in the ways of another culture at a time when that culture or nation was under scrutiny, or had the western gaze upon it and had to answer for itself in an accessible and heart-tugging manner, and that westerners will accept literature from far-off nations if said books reduce complex issues to the level of sentimental manipulation and utilise a stripped-down prose style dripping with enough faux-literariness so that it reads like "well-crafted and deeply felt" literature; Marcus said it was nearing his bedtime and he should probably hit the sack, and thanks for the wine.

On Reading

Readers & Their Fates

I N THE WORKSHOP, I offered the following overview: "In my experience, there are six kinds of readers. The first aspire to omnilegence, i.e. to have read and absorbed all worthwhile books in existence, leaping with hopeless indiscrimination from a lesser title in Zola's Rougon-Macquart sequence, to a Stewart Home novel with a non-provocative title, to a former rock musician's valiant first-novel failure, to an obscure 1000-page Zimbabwean epic about crooked agribusiness, to an elegiac Frank Kermode memoir. The second are strategically rapacious, selecting the crème of an oeuvre, skipping the minor works in favour of a realistic overview of one school of writing: for example, with the French decadents, tackling the central authors (Huysmans, Mirbeau, Verlaine), skipping the more marginal figures (Schwob, Montesquiou, de Gourmont), or with the Dickens canon, sidestepping such filler as *Barnaby Rudge*, *Dombey and Son*, and *The Old Curiosity Shop*. The third are the careful sluggards, reading fewer books per annum than the first two, choosing an eclectic mix from various periods, schools, and presses, making them knowledgeable about a wide range of essential texts. The fourth are the occasional toe-dippers, taking on a classic from time to time, sticking to more digestible and popular fare, preferring their pages plot-packed and readable, i.e. easier to finish over the course of a month. The fifth are the one-bookers: people who select a novel (if a classic, *Jane Eyre* or *Great Expectations*), to read, and prolong the process over a full annum, sometimes not even finishing the text. The sixth are the one-bookers who read the latest bestseller and rave about this one book to colleagues, friends, and family for the whole annum, until the next one comes around, and repeat the revolting cycle until death. These are the six reader classifications."

This provoked further contemplations about the aleatory nature of reading. How one man can walk the planet and never crack open *Don Quixote*, how one woman can enjoy a century of existence, and never read a sentence of *Roderick Random*. It made me wonder about all the novels I enshrine, and their strange pathways through time. Has President Obama ever muscled through *Tristram Shandy*, including endnotes? Has Black Francis of Pixies read W.G. Sebald's *The Emigrants*? Has Paul McCartney ever chortled at Lucy Ellmann? How much Ali Smith has Patti Smith read, and how much Zadie Smith has Patti Smith read, and how much Stevie Smith have they all read? Has that one cool dude on the underground reading Perec's *Things* ever lost himself in Roubaud's *Great Fire of London*? Is there a life-changing novel making an orbit round the world towards me that will, by fluke of chance, be purchased by someone else ten minutes before I arrive at the book shop? Is there, beneath that pile of books stacked up in the corner, an obscure author's forgotten masterpiece, waiting to be unearthed? How many not-quite-right books do I plough through in place of the perfect ones that might forever elude my eyes? Why do certain books arrive at the wrong time in one's life, and find themselves forever blacklisted? Why do books once rapturously received collapse upon second readings? Do books have a life after that one rapturous reading? How can it be one person's lot to only finish reading Stephen King's *The Stand* in the course of their lives, and another's to read the entire pantheon of Boxall-approved world classics from Homer to now?

Should a reader have a "conscience" about what is read in their lifetimes? Does someone serious about literature have an obligation to read the books less conscientious readers will never think to pick up? Or is the reader, regardless of their powers, allowed to read whatever takes their fancy, neglecting lesser-known books in favour of franchise sci-fi or other popular brands? There are readers with degrees in literature who, upon graduating and moving in to their non-literary professions, spend their lives reading franchise books, having "tackled" the classics in their late teens. There are readers whose large intellects take them into taxing occupations, leaving them so frazzled in the evening, the first novel reached for is something light and brainless, like the works of Toby Litt. There are readers who, seduced by the lure of the zeitgeist, snack on the latest craze in book, film, and music, in a desperate need to be included in the often vapid and boring public discourse. These are readers who, capable of tackling *Ulysses* or other "difficult" books, wimp out and watch boxsets.

There is no public pressure on intelligent people to read widely, indiscriminately, and madly. In Britain, the most popular outlets for literature are focused on middlebrow novels from large publishers. There are few programmes or articles appreciating the works of hundreds of past masters, because of their "limited appeal." The reader is never pushed into eclecticism. On BBC Radio 4, the tone of literature programmes is one of "reading is fun," and that all literature is equal. Kafka, George R.R. Martin, Proust, Ian Rankin . . . there is no difference. It's all reading. Reading is awesome. Councils and libraries, with their events, are continually promoting events with authors dragged up through their awards schemes, initiatives, awards: a cosy ecosystem allowing for the safe collaboration between companies and councils, keeping the agenda safe and unprovocative. Logging on to the Edinburgh International Book Festival, one of the first things I saw promoted: an evening with Jeffrey Archer.

Enough said.

19

"Y<small>OU MET</small> Raine?"

"Hence the hangover."

"You peep his collection of first editions?"

"No."

"You went to Raine Upright's cottage and you never saw his first editions?"

"I believe that's been established."

"That man might be a shameless swizzle lover, and a Carlisle Brass M47 Solid Victorian Fingertip knob, but one of his virtues is the prize collection of strokable, lickable, suckable, and nibblable hardbacks he keeps at room temperature in a room. He's also an author. He trades in literary misanthropy, making megabucks shilling mope to the masses. In *100 Novels that Should be Fisted to Death*, he performs smarter-than-thou eviscerations of lit staples like *Sense & Sensibility* and *To Kill a Mockingbird*. Here's his take on the latter."

> This overly praised, overly adored "classic" shamelessly plays the race card at every opportunity. To declare a hatred of this novel is to slap every black man and woman in the face.

"Ha."

"It's a lucrative market, literature for people who hate literature."

"F'real?"

"Yes. People who like the idea of being well-read readers but resent having to actually read. Books like Upright's allow frustrated readers a place to simultaneously stoke their hatred of literature while reading something."

"F'ed up."

"Indeedio. My experience as a librarian proves to me that a huge number of people who read books resent the act. I see depressed loners, widows, and the pitifully unattractive checking out romances, sci-fis, or

52

literary texts well beyond their intellectual reach, and I know from the sagging hearts in evidence these books are a means to avoid the void. They offer a mild panacea to the daily torment that is their lives, and resent that these books can't find them lovers, bring back their husbands, or rearrange their faces into more pleasing shapes. The book therefore becomes a mere reminder of that inadequacy, like daily medication or a nightly slug of wine, and therefore an item of resentment."

"But literature exists to administer a sort of morphine for the soul."

"For such chumps as us and I perchance, but I am speaking about people who lack the emotional and mental training who need books to offer more immediate relief. There should be a range of lit targeted at depressed widows and whonot, not all this romance nonsense offering lame escape. The trouble is, writers of literature are under pressure to appeal to the emotions by perpetually writing about birth, love, death, and so on. Most popular novels simply must offer profound soundbytes, hard-won reflections on loss, love, death, everything has to be fucking EPIC, or it simply won't do. These poor bastards should have stories about people who need four valiums to rise in the morning, never mind about people who overcome all their problems. When did literature become such a slave to the feel-good fallacy?"

"Isn't art about exploding the everyday, not claustrophobisizing?"

"Come, laddie! Remember what Lord Sorrentino said? Art cannot save anybody from anything. Anyway, this Upright guy has grown to hate literature. There's no other explanation. He rails against the so-called middlebrow masses, but you never hear him singing the praises of any of his beloved obscures."

"You two have met?"

"We were lovers for a spell. I made him cockaleekie soup while he sprawled on the sofa pontificating on the moral poison of John Gardner."

"What—"

"His penis is small and ineffective. I only permitted him penetration twice, and after his failure to sing the praises of Alex Kovacs's

A Currency of Paper, H.G. Wells's *The First Men in the Moon*, Kurt Vonnegut's *Deadeye Dick*, Michael Westlake's *The Utopian*, William H. Gass's *Middle C*, Graham Rawle's *Women's World*, Julian Rios's *Larva: A Midsummer Night's Babel*, Boris Vian's *Heartsnatcher*, Tom Whalen's *The President in Her Towers*, and Kelly Link's *Magic for Beginners*, I kicked him to the kirk. But I agreed with his position on Philip Roth. He can't be blamed for his horny-ass novels. People want the same things from their books. Titillation. Everyone, if honest, would end up writing *Sabbath's Theater*, because in the end, the rubbing of our genitals at various angles is the only real pleasure we have in life."

20

THE EMAIL EXCHANGE with Ledgie had apotheosizzled. Ledgie had threatened to "mash the Marcal mush" with a bowling ball, and Marcus talked about totting an AK47 around the island and firing upon "human mollusks in Porsches," and Ledgie repeated that Marcus had inherited the hovel having signed the papers, and that if he complained again, a team of unkind rugger-lovers would use their hot towels to flick him into the realm of acceptance of the realm of being screwed from top to tail. Marcus howled vowels into the wind: "Aaaaaeeeeeeeooooooo." Having witnessed this vocal crumple into despair from the window, Isobel was satisfied that Marcus's pain would cure his Island Denial, and force him into cultivating a "character" on the island to help retain his sanity. She convinced him to meet her parents who occupied a mobile home perched on a cliff on the Broch of Borwick.

The Senior Bartmels, two clerks having sunk into lives of hohum-drumness, removed themselves from the "bustle" of Kirkwall and holed up in a plastic rectangle powered by gas cylinders to watch the soothing Atlantic from their windows, earning the status of beloved eccentrics. Their mobile, named The Dangler for its precarious perchment on an eroding cliff-face, was clad in reinforced PVC tarpaulin and creosoted a vibrant rust-brown. "I was raised in the cottage until fourteen, where-after the flit," Isobel said. "During periods of extremely low wind pres-sure, and once the supporting beams I begged them to erect were in place, I slept in the mobile to lance the loneliness. Their 'characters' have been established. Fifteen years later, the Bartmels are still a talk-ing point in the bars when conversation dries up. 'D'you reckon that Dangler will fall into the Broch this year?' and the like. I couldn't care less. The fact is, coastal erosion has been minimal in that period, and will not affect them in their lifetimes, so this pub-craved catastrophe is a dream. The threat comes from howling winds. I will pitch to them for the ninth time this month the installation of safety buffers."

Mr. Bartmel, a hunched beanpole, appeared in an apron that read: Daddy Dangler, Head Chef. His humming rhubarb cheeks betrayed traces of his former life as a swizzler-lover. He hugged his daughter with exaggerated oomph. The mother was sitting on the wraparound couch reading an issue of *Time* magazine on Angela Merkel. The parents had carved a career escorting tourists around the Broch, in addition to a cup of tea and a hug for £2 a pop. Isobel knew her father worked for a content-writing firm most of the day, but accepted the illusion that they made their money from being cliff freaks. The mobile home interior was standard: sofa (living room), beside a small serving area (kitchen), with a series of cubicles containing beds (bedrooms), and a makeshift toilet (bathroom).

"Marcus: meet the parental unit," Isobel said. Don Bartmel slapped Marcus pal-like on the shoulder.

"Marcustard! Marcustodian! Welcome to Shedz Bartmel. I am Donald Bartmel the First and I have at present five rashers sizzling on a Teflon. Come sit on the comfort. Here's a wife I have. Her name's Erin."

Erin Bartmel removed the *Time* from her face and forced a lethal smile onto her lips, her arm outstretched in a violent proffer. "I have learned that Angela Merkel used to bond atoms. Perfect training for German Chancellor! Hello, I'm Erin Bartmel. I am the Elected Chairwoman of this Caravan." Marcus, unprepared for the blitz of quirk, mumbled a sedate hello upon sitting. Don served him bacon on a brioche and explained in his own words their decision to flee the Kirkwall bustle.

"You ever step into a snare that snaps off your foot, Marcustomer? You ever inhale a cocktail of carbon monoxide and osmium tetroxide, Marcurial? Life in Kirkwall was like being crushed over a period of years between two enclosing walls. I said to the wife I have, I said Erin we must leave this metaphorical oblivion and move to teeter on the edge of actual oblivion. At least that's more interesting!"

"Yes," the wife Don had added, "so we bought The Dangler and set up over the beautiful Broch. How's the brioche?"

"Good."

On Writing

The Launch

D URING THE teaching stint, I began to suffer from unpleasant nightmares in the form of a second-by-second replay of my first book launch.

Launching in public the first novel I published was an appalling mistake, and one of the most regrettable experiences of my life. I had written a novel entitled *Fat Battlements*, a satirical wartime comedic romp, taking sideswipes at so-called Islamic State, svelte lunatic Bashar al-Assad, Boris Johnson's unamusing novel *Seventy Two* [sic] *Virgins*, the West's persistent trading in illegal arms, and Australian chat show host Andrew Denton, alongside chapters in which the author waxes on writing the novel and its predicted reception, published by small independent house Three Quid Stereo. I chose to have a launch for the novel at local boho arts venue The Aphid Tippler: a place where slumming art students named Tristram serve ironic falafel and Mexican bean soup at their own pace, shruggish bit-part actresses serve organic root beer to their inferiors in ill-shaped beakers with visible resentment, the homeless mingle in awkward disunion with "artisans" and "intellectuals," and assorted "poets" and "performers" broadcast their latest efforts to an indifferent room.

At The Aphid Tippler, the clientele like to surround themselves with "creatives," either to subsume that inventiveness into their otherwise unoriginal lives, to convince themselves they are a part of some nascent "scene," as in the famous pre-war cafés of Vienna or Paris, and to talk at length about the countless projects "on the go" that remain unopened on laptops for weeks, spiralling into months, into years. These people prefer to have that "creativity" as a background noise, never listening to the words being spoken and their attempted meanings, but to talk over the speaker with more important matters, such as what middlebrow author's works they are currently reading, their unbiased take on politics from a moral highground up on the moon, or whatever more famous performer they intend to see, whose art, having been approved in *Flavour Wire*, *The Skinny*, and *The A.V. Club*, will be viewed with reverence. Not seeking the public's fake-polite tolerance, I had chosen on purpose a venue where the public would speak over my readings, making a point about the attitude the public have towards struggling artists, while not worrying about making a spectacle of myself.

This proved a mistake, as the choice had a lasting impact on my friendships and relationship with Alice Rìos. I opened the evening with a self-deprecating monologue explaining that while I was pleased some people had attended this launch, I was on the whole opposed to the notion of an author launching their works: as a disciple of Barthes, I would rather nix the author from all literary production and have a free-floating readerly utopia removed from the commodification of personality, but that I was capitulating to the pressures of the marketplace, and certain well-meaning people (a nod to Alice, sulking in the corner), by appearing in public. The guests resented this "begrudging" attitude, believing that I should be more appreciative that they had showed up at all, which was true.

"We don't mind if you knock off, mate!" Paul Appleby, a friend's spouse, unwittily remarked. This was to receive the biggest laugh of the night. I began by reading from the piquant pastiche of Boris Johnson's *Seventy Two* [sic] *Virgins*, a section I thought might elicit more chuckles for its overt mocking of the blonde political schemer's flat prose. After the reading, to which the guests responded with bafflement— interrupted when the waitress asked loudly: "WHO ORDERED THE MUSHROOM, SPINACH, AND FAVA BEAN SMOOTHIE?", to which one man responded loudly, "MOI!", eliciting chuckles from his friends, as though I wasn't stood there, reading work I had laboured on for years—I stepped from the stage and proceeded with the mingling portion of the evening.

First to appreciate me: Thom Gordons, whom I had tolerated as a postgrad student, and whose smarm I was having to tolerate now. One of my rivals, I had feared his publication ahead of mine, and scowled as his post-gender historical novel, *The Womanman's Daughterson*, set in a Victorian brothel, was snapped up by Canongate, and reviewed by Michel Faber in *The Guardian*, who said: "I read in a state of violent envy that a writer this young could command such an explosive talent." Thom had behaved from the beginning as a man aware that his prose would command large audiences, and that one day, he would be called upon to sit next to Mariella Frostrup at the Edinburgh Book Festival and make right-on remarks about gender politics to a loving audience of BuzzFeeders. I had behaved from the beginning as a man aware that his prose would command a handful of readers, most of them friends of the author, who would read his strange self-conscious meanderings, referring to himself in a show of remarkable disconnection from the realities of the literary marketplace, and that one day, when called upon to tout his wares in public, would wriggle from the responsibility, and cite Barthes as an intellectual rationale for being a colossal pussy. A mutual realisation of this fact was present in Thom's words: "Great stuff, man." (At Thom's launch I had spent the night in the corner, batting off Alice's violent insistence that I shove through a huddle of admirers to force out a congratulations, and part with £16.99 for a pre-signed hardback).

Next, my mother, who offered a hug and polite well-done. This masked her real sentiments, later expressed: "It's all very well, writing this look-at-me stuff, moaning to the reader about how put-upon you are, but the fact is: you've boxed yourself into this problem. If you wrote a straightforward story, and now, I know, I know, you don't want to hear this. But we're only trying to help." (Alice was present at this anti-anti-mainstream harangue, having made her thoughts on "metawank" clear). "Alice has told me about Jasper Fforde, have you heard of him? He writes these books about other books in the form of detective novels. And he ensures a broad appeal by writing about popular classics, like in *The Eyre Affair*. You could try something like this. You like Dosto-evsky, don't you? Why don't you write about some sort of murder taking place at a Dostoevsky conference, something that parallels the murder in *Crime and Punishment*?" (This was Alice's idea.) She added: "And at that launch, I have to say, I thought opening with that stuff about how it pained you to be there was unfair on everyone, I mean, they made the effort to come out and see you, and you say to their faces, I am basically above doing this, but will deign to step off my lofty perch and speak to you. Is that the sort of way you treat people? I never raised you to be like that."

Then followed: Penelope Elappe, a well-meaning spinster at work on two Harlequin romances, in whose eyes I observed kind-natured sympathy; Driscoll Hamfutzer, a science writer in whose eyes I observed barely concealed mockery; Vince Armoire, someone I had added on LinkedIn, in whose eyes I observed a bobbing impatience to bag a copy and pen his mediocre Amazon review; Tom Bobbins, an online friend I had pretended to like for seven years, in whose eyes I observed the slow replacement of long-sustained adoration with burning disap-pointment; Harold Opus, a wry academic, in whose eyes I observed patronising faked amusement; Carol Hacker, the mother of an ex-lover, in whose eyes I read the usual inappropriate consideration when I had long ago severed ties with her daughter; Dennis Friel, a friend in whose eyes I read a staggering lack of interest in the novel in favour of the free booze; Anna Lopez, a friend in whose eyes I read an impatience for the attention to shift from me and back to her and her travel anecdotes; Bo-ril Soxmond, a friend in whose eyes I read a sense of infinite sadness, that after so long striving for success as a writer, this limp offering was the best I could muster as a debut. In the public, inconvenienced at hav-ing to nudge past the modest thrum of my success, I read loathing that my publishing victory should prevent their easy access to the till to pay for their elderflower cordial and halloumi salads.

The evening fizzled into drunken self-triumph, and the nurturing of new resentments for the perceived reactions of all those in attendance, plus a catalogue of peevishness at those who couldn't be bothered to turn up.

Alice Rìos had criticised my adversarial approach to friendships. There is no better test of loyalty, however, than publishing a novel. She berated me for inserting the names of friends at choice moments: a tactic to prove if my friends had read the novel from cover to cover, skipped parts, or not read anything at all. Alice believed the reader reserved the right to skim or not read as was their wont and that a true friend had no need to "test" their friendship in such a sly manner. I believe in a strong code of conduct with friends' novels: I read them from cover to cover, even if the content turns me puce with rage, and even if I despise the novel, I will serve up a four-star review in praise, faking compliments about the prose if there was nothing commendable. The experiment proved worthwhile: the friends who had bought the novel never commented on their own cameos, which wasn't sure-fire proof that they hadn't read the whole thing, but the rarity of finding one's name inserted into a published novel was surely worth a comment of assent to the author, but none came.

"Perhaps they read the section, intended to comment, then forgot by the end," Alice said.

"Please. If I inserted you into a novel, you would react with puzzlement, annoyance, or elation. You would say *something*."

"If you were irked, you might not bring it up. It might have been exposed as an embarrassing attempt to shame people you assumed were your friends."

"Nah. They no read."

"Perhaps there's a reason they don't contact you as much as before the launch?"

"Hmm."

"Plus. What sort of friend makes it a condition of that friendship that they *must* read a novel that might not even interest them?"

"If my friends don't even read my novels, who will?"

I put Alice's criticisms to one side and compiled a list of the no-shows. To them, I sent the following email:

Dear [name],

Recently, I launched my new novel, *Fat Battlements*, at The Aphid Tippler. I noticed that in spite of a promise you would attend, you did not show up at the launch. Having a novel released in this ultra-competitive, marketing-obsessed publishing climate is an achievement of immense proportions, esp. one as self-indulgent and up its own posterior as mine, so by not showing up to this event, this one moment of glory I permitted myself, you have placed me in a horrendous position. Those among you who would consider me an acquaintance buried in the past, irrelevant to your current lives, I can understand your non-attendance, and make no criticisms of your decision. I wish you well, as we tread our different paths. Those among you with whom I am in semi-regular correspondence, and who have been following me in my writing career, and hence would not consider yourself "indifferent" to my progress, it is harder for me not to take your non-attendance as a personal snub. Of course, there are the usual probable excuses: long-standing plans for that night, a cold/other illness, problems at home, and so on. The most probable reason is that the launch was too far away, and you simply didn't value our semi-friendship enough to make the trek to support me. I take this as an off-the-cuff rebuff. I will not be attending or supporting any of your future events, if this is the level of value you place on my career. And finally, the people I had considered proper "friends" who were not in attendance, please consider our "friendships" over. Not attending this launch is akin to kick in the testes with a spike-encrusted jackboot. It is akin to slapping me in the cheek with a pox-ridden glove. It is akin to pummelling my sister with rocks on her birthday. It is akin to stripping the fur from my beloved kitten. It is akin . . . ah, thought I was about to launch into another interminable list, were we? You need worry no longer, I am releasing you from the burden of being my "friend," since it appears such a strain having to enter one room for an hour to support me. Goodbye forever.

Yours,

Ex-Friend

21

Topics discussed: the preference of brioche over brown bread except in the case of hardboiled eggs (on toast); Don's appendectomy from the perspective of a Bulgarian immigrant in for chemo on his cancerous lungs; the wisdom of investing in additional wind defences in the event of a second Hurricane Jemima; Erin's newfound appreciation for the South American otter following a recent BBC2 documentary; the nature of Marcus's undertaking and the painful inheritance of a damp moss-ridden cottage as the site for its occurrence; Isobel's couch as a temporary refuge before the (impossible) upcoming repair works; Don's previous career as an underling at Malcolm Hatchie's underwriting firm in Stromness; the continual battle to receive 4G from EE while perched off the edge of a cliff; the suicidal souls saved by Don and Erin with a shot of TLC and TCP; Isobel's amusement at Marcus's physical awkwardness and his failure to carve a "character" for himself on the island; Don's suggestion that Marcus install himself as a "reader in residence" at the Broch of Gurness and offer reading tips to tourists; Erin's reminder that Raine Upright had tried that in 2003 and was forced to perch off the Historic Scotland site on a designated rock at a near-fatal angle; the nights Isobel spent begging her parents to return to the cottage and minister to her childhood; the year-long silent sulk of protest; the realisation that her parents were happier and more alive precipissing around than in their whole lives, and Isobel's acceptance of their weirdness; Erin's morning sprints along the Broch and her Orkney marathon record of two hours nine minutes; the opinion that man (and woman) was not made to live in stifling cities and that theirs was the only freedom; Isobel's struggle to secure Marcus a library card under the Highland Council "no visitors" clause, requiring at least two years residence before a book might be withdrawn; the persistence of crows in trying to steal Don's haggis and ale pie; the reminder to fit wind defences within a week or meet the wrath of Isobel.

22

"WHY, WHY, WHY, Marcus Simon Schott, are you here, you fuck-ing nitwit? I came here to read. You came here to read!? Then what the hell are you doing sleeping with some spindle-shanked librar-ian and supping weak tea in her parents' caravan? You are supposed to be holed up in a room reading Amos Tutuola and J.M. Coetzee. Not carving out some sort of 'life' here . . . 'life' comes after the reading is complete! YOU HAVE BEEN OVER THIS! I know, I know, I know, this wasn't meant to happen. I am soaked to the knees in trouble. And that is another thing. All the people here don't speak right. They talk in language fitting to their 'characters.' What is this 'character' shite? Is it so terrible here that people need to transform themselves into ex-aggerated loons who speak in some wacky literary babble? And about this Isobel. She's fine, she's fine, she's no Sandra Acer, but I need her to keep me in food and warmth. I've been here three weeks and I haven't read enough. I'm falling behind. Goddamn it mate, you have 997 books left to read. I know, I know, I can't concentrate, this Ledgie business is fucking with my head. I read and read but my thoughts flee to vi-sions of skewering Ledgie in the nostrils. I need a long-term plan. A new long-term plan is what I needed. OK, Marcus. Cogi-fucking-tate. How about this. Propose to Isobel. No, that's insane. That's lunatic. Or I could work for Mr. Upright as a bookkeeper? No, I can't work. I need to leech off Isobel. I have no other option. Look at the fucking place. Look at the rotting stinking mildewing horror of the place. I need to move in with Isobel and sit on the couch reading while she's working in the library, and then three or probably four years later, I can wangle a divorce and move back home. You can't treat people like that. I know, I know, I can't . . . perhaps the marriage will dissolve, perhaps she'll ap-preciate a husband who keeps his mouth shut and reads non-stop. No, this is mental. I don't even . . . I mean the shagging is pleasant . . . I'm not in love with her . . . oh, I need to get out of here, I need some ad-vice," Marcus said to himself walking around the cottage for the final time.

On Reading

Various Positions

"WHAT IS the best position in which to sit while reading?" I asked the workshop. No response. "Let me offer a brief skillet of nous. First: never supine. That means flatbacked. This position creates awkward crickage of neck and a blood-rush to the head. You might think the blood flowing towards the brain might help in following literature's complex circuitry. You are at risk of clot and migraines, and in the case of Brian Grappa of Aberdeenshire, a cerebral haemorrhage at the age of 27. This Oblomovian mook spent an annum backflat reading Cornish poetics and wound up at the crematorium before kissing his first female. Learn from this. No supine. Next. Sitting upright in a wooden chair? Never. Your schoolteachers might have planted this anti-slump seed: the belief that uprightness is essential to learning. Not so. Those fifteen-plus anna spent in education have fuzzed the real. Reading in a chair, with the book propped up on a table, is uncomfortable, liable to cause spinal caries, and in the case of Eleni Xanthappe of Inverness-shire, a complete severing of the spine at the age of 24. This Grecian poetess spent half an ann upright reading treatises on Aristophanes, and wound up sinking into the sod in a pine box. Learn from this. No upright. Next. Stood up or in motion. Fools! Reading stood up causes a swift stoop, and in motion causes neck ache and risk of being bus-smashed. Take Bill Ho of Ross-shire, who read while waiting for trains and buses, and ended up hunchbacked at the age of 21, so stooped that one morning he toppled onto the train tracks. This bibliophilic Bill ended up bagged, binned, and hosed off Scotrail property, before he had even squizzed a supermoon. And take Lou Mulch of Doss-shire, a walk-reader who couldn't crick his neck upwards in time to avoid an oncoming bus. This restless leg-end ended up front-splat on the 43 at the age of 18. Learn from this. No stood up or in motion. Reading on the bed? You think that's safe? Nope. Sure, no risk of slow death. However, it has been proven that reading on the bed is too comfortable, and one's mind enters a pre-sleep mode, meaning words on the page are being read but not understood. Reading becomes skimming. Take Imp Collagen of Saussure-shire, who read her GSCE texts on the bed. Come exam time, not a single recollection of a book-word arrived in her cranium. This studious loafer ended up with five fails at the age of 15, and spends her life mopping up pooch piss at the local canine café. Learn from this. Next. The proper: locate a comfortable wing chair and sit in a semi-upright but well-supported position with one cushion if required. You will slump during the course of the read so remember to right yourself every several minutes to prevent sinking into a bed-like torpor. Now, we also need to address the problem of hardbacks. A hardback packs more heft than its soft counterpart. To prevent the sort of wrist trauma that befell Tim Sardine of Shyreshire, whose wrists snapped off one Wednesday after reading hardback after hardback without the proper support. This adventurous tome-tackler ended up handless at the age of 12, and abandoned reading forever, before he had even tickled a Tillman. To remedy the hardback cramp, it is permissible to prop one's lower extremities on a foot stool and raise the hardback nearer to the eyes by placing it atop two cushions, allowing these to take the weight. Correct."

23

HATE ERUPTED at The Swaddled Firkin between a connoisseur of the Pineapple Pulveriser and Raine Upright. His après-lunch tipples had blossomed over the months from the slow supping of a Cranberry Catastrophe while red-penning the *Times Literary Supplement* to the swift necking of several random swizzles while scribbling crazed responses in the margins of the *New Yorker* and *McSweeney's*. Arnold Bleu was a local writer who had formed a Dave Eggers fanclub on the island in an attempt to publish his "proto-noir fictionickle" "Slice of Knife" in *McSweeney's Quarterly Concern*, a publisher of the sort of fiction that made Raine Upright sit upright and rain blows upon the page. Bleu spoke about the "important moral lessons" in Eggers's "adult and serious" novels. Raine called Eggers a "perm-haired zeitgeist-licking twot," and Bleu hurled a Pulveriser at Raine's left cheek. Raine flounced out the bar howling a negative review of *You Shall Know Our Velocity!* and bumped into Marcus.

"Fantastic, more middlebrow arseholes! I suppose you find Dave Eggers the spokesman of the fucking Gen-ZXY crowd?!"

"Who? I came for a chat."

"A chat? Fine, provided you make no statements like 'Zadie Smith blends the robust satire of Martin Amis with the studied social science of E.M. Forester' or suchlike shitterooney, all right? Onward to The Crabbed Satchel."

This being a tavern serving thimbles numbered roman numerically, each increasing in alcohol content up to the fatal Thimble X, taken only when an alcoholic had written consent from his GP to euthanise himself.

"The man who took the thimble that soaked the liver that killed the heart that smack built was Marshall Suite. He was raised among druggies. Sad tale. I won't tell it here, I can't abide harsh realism."

"I need advice."

"Don't read J.G. Bollard. That's my advice. Sure, those clinical novels like *Crash* and *Concrete Island* seem cool with their polymorphous perversities, their whiffs of semen and engine coolant. But the man punched a clock. 'Mr Ballard, can we have your far-seeing vision of a civilisation turned bestial because of roads by March 10?' 'Mr Ballard, can you set your dystopia in a shopping centre, and have Drummond eating a hamster this time?' Corporate man. Family man. As radical as your mum's crumpets."

"No, not on Ballard. I—"

"And forget that book-shitting machine John Updick. A perfect example of tireless productivity yielding no value. His routine: up at six to cart about walled greens and whack a ball into a far-off hole, an hour primping his hairy caterpillars in the mirror, then into the study around eight to try, for the fortieth time, to elevate the uninteresting lives of breadbasket shaggers and WASPs to the status of art."

"No, not on Updike. I—"

"Avoid Douglas Coupbland. A man who leeches on the now. His creative process: 'The internet is a thing happening in the world. I will write a novel about how that impacts on people.' 'School shootings are in the news. I will write a novel about how that impacts on people.' 'Social media sites on the internet are mentioned often. I will write a novel about how that impacts on people. And so people can understand me, and I can sell copies, I will cram a zillion cultural references into the text.'"

"No, not on Coupland. I—"

"A final piece of advice, sidestep *McSweeney's*, onto a landmine if need be. Have you ever encountered a periodical more achingly eager to please while simultaneously feigning a pose of cool nonchalance? Hey, like us or hate us, whatever, but you will probably like us, because we have a natty line in cool-dude humour, and content tailored to please the middlingest of the middlebrow, and nothing that will remotely offend. Our stories are all written in simple English and are about American families coping with loss in a post-9/11 America. And hey, we have cool cartoonists! And endearing felt hardbacks. Love us!"

"No. I want advice about marriage. I am planning to propose to Isobel."

"Bartmel?! That balmy chaffinch? I need an IV for that at least."

Raine ordered two IVs from the expressionless pudding at the bar: Mrs. Glomp, the silent owner who had been advised never to speak a word to her clientele in the event someone collapsed in her premises after one or two VIIIs. The tavern had three drinking divisions—a I–III for new customers, the IV–VI section for regulars, a VI–IX section for alcoholics, and a quiet corner for the X tipplers, positioned near the fire exit so the ambulance service could remove the corpses without disturbing the others.

"So you want to marry Isobat Fartmel. I can emphatically advise you there: no shitting way, Markie-poops. Not unless you want the Fartmel wings flapping at you every day, every night. I courted Fartmel for a month. She wanted access to my rare books library, her quim the price of admission. There are women on this island, Markie-polyp, women who drop their keks in a minim at the prospect of an original 1865 *Alice*. I own that. In addition to an original 1853 of Charlotte Brontë's *Villette*. Speaking of the Brontës, you know Anne was actually the talented one? Sure, Charlotte's ludicrous Gothic romances and Emily's piece of tawdry chick-lit steal the limelight, but in *The Tenant of Wildfell Hall*, she rolls out this fat polemic on the human rights abuses evident in Victorian marriage laws, and suckerpunches the crooked establishment. And in *Agnes Gray*, she captures the excruciating dullness of life as a sexless governess for a family of titled wankers. Anyway, back to Isaboke."

"Since I lost my cottage, which I lost the very moment I arrived here, I need somewhere to stay, where I can read all day, without interruptions."

"Oh, Markie-poke, I feel the knowing. Fnow the kneel . . . *burp!* . . . excusez-moi. Now, let's list the pros of Izzie weddage: the broad is book bats. If you imbibliobibe, you will remain her bibliobaby, OK?

The cons: sitting in that sinking shed with those two fruitcocks, mimi and pipi, and their bacon on brioche, every Sunday, for up to five hours. And forget having opinions, that bint loves all ink on pulp unconditztionally, right? I once slapped that plane-hopping hack Paul Theroux and she flung a melon at my face. She wouldn't even let me sink my meathooks into that smug infidel Richard Dorkings. So yes, my friend, if you intend to nail that millenary, become Izzybat's little bibliobitch. How's your IV?"

"I've only had a drip."

"This tipple makes me piss like a water cannon."

"Nice."

"Thanks. They call that Rabelaisian humour, little Markie-putz."

"Do they."

"Now, lemme tell you about that caviller Michel Houellebecq."

24

"Yes Mum, I am engaged to be married."
(I can't believe it either).

"No, this isn't a hoax."
(Or is it?)

"Yes, we are very much in love."
(I'm in love with her sofa and fridge and heating).

"No, I sold the cottage."
(For free to termites and roaches).

"We're having a low-key ceremony."
(Everyone in her family, none from mine).

"I asked her over a candle-lit dinner at Orkney's top restaurant."
(In the kitchen while she was making beans on toast).

"She was ecstatic."
(She said all right, on the condition I provide her with a child).

"I am over the moon."
(I'm terrified and have no idea what I'm doing).

"No, we're staying here."
(Because returning to unemployed life in the city is unbearable, or is this worse . . . ?)

"We will visit."
(No we won't).

"Yes, my reading is going well."
(Four books in three months. Astronomical online delivery fees. No library card in sight. No access to Raine's library. Barely anything in Isobel's shelves on my list. Running out of cash. Can't concentrate).

"It should be completed on time."
(At the last estimate, in about ten to twelve years).

"Yes, we will probably have a baby."
(That being the one and only reason for the marriage on her side).

"Yes, I'm eating well!"
(Beans. Soup. Oven chips).

"I'm looking forward to a new life here."
(Scared shitless and have no idea what to expect).

25

ISOBEL, HAVING exhausted the island's bachelor market and found the produce unsavoury, confessed to a certain strain of desperation in her hunt for a mate. She insisted upon someone who endeavoured to read two to three books per week as the one unwavering criteria. This led her to Bob McGills, kind-hearted stutterer and toper of nine science-fiction epics per fortnight. Having stripped McGills of his long-standing virginity, she helped him flourish into an adult male not forever clinging to his shirt sleeves, struggling to enunciate Ns, and ranking the best Doctor Whos in order starting with Tom Baker, but into a man committed to his responsibilities as assistant manager at Asda and volunteer work at the shelter. This left him no time for books. She moved on to Des Fritch, co-editor of *The Island Oracle*, a handmade magazine exploring popular conspiracy theories, such as that the opening of the Stromness Tesco was responsible for unleashing satan on the island, that Mine Howe is haunted by the spirit of a greengrocer asphyxiated on the site in 1969, and at certain times faint murmurings of "parsnips!" could be heard, and that the force of David Icke's consciousness powered the climate, resulting in tempestuous fluctuations in weather. This lasted a week. She moved on to man named "G," a performance artist who hacked up the novels of Sven Hassel and pasted them to his naked body, leaping around the Broch of Gurness in erotically provocative configurations as the tourists were walking in to see the remains of a Pictish village. Among the other lovers: Terence Walnous, an Orcadian "purist" who spat at anyone who read anything other than the works of George Mackay Brown; David Cashau, a vicar whose penchant for reciting passages from William Burroughs during sermons lost him 45% of his congregation and hastened his return to telemarketing; Gareth Chestnaut, a former newspaper hack writing a ten-volume series on the Princess Diana conspiracy based on a new eyewitness account from a French pedestrian passing the Fiat Uno that evening; Roman Hazelouf, a tiler and poet with a £20,000 Scottish arts stipend working on his first Gaelic collection *Tha am mullach ag eu-dìon*; Liam Peampt, a farmer ploughing through *War & Peace* one page per day; Simon Pistachous, a children's entertainer whose positive write-up in *The Orkney Herald* forced him to drink to cope with the pressure; Frank Pecarff, a supermarket manager with a fascination for the occult who was sad to receive Ambrose Bierce's *The Devil's Dictionary* and find a mere list of inaccurate and self-loathing definitions; and so on.

As she told her friend Jane Clothnapper: "This male is no exemplar of maleness. I have parlezvoused with a parlour of parlous poseurs and porous men-brains: this Marcus is a sparse specimen. But I'm a specimentalist: I'm a whirligirl who makes men whirligag. I have to confess the Comstockian appeal has come to a stock-stand-still. He's more like Winston these days, complaining about the unsmooth shavery of my Venus Divine razors, and the exercise I encourage him to perform. I'm a big bother. And I will let you into a secret: I'm already pregnant. I'm about to kill him with slow daughter torture. Anyway, Clothnapper, I lime-cordially invite you to our pending wedding. Yes, St. Magnus Cathedral. No, I intend to wear a polka-dotted shirt with a small unbuttoned blue cardigan. I want the rest of the female attendees to wear wedding dresses, for them to be seated beside men, and for them to kiss instead of us. We'll shake hands or bump navels or something when the priest sez. Yes, I am stretching my 'character' a little, but I have a reputation to uphold, lovey!"

On Writing

Scenic Views

I N ORKNEY, I tried to make the most of the scenic views. That summer, as most summers, the scenic views had been monopolised by the tourists. I spent two hours motoring from one car park to another, pipped by a Volvo S40 at each spot. One day, after sneaking into an available space, I met the horn-blasting wrath of a family of four, paid £15 for the parking and entered the queue to see shards of pottery in glass cases. Inside the museum, unimpressed children ran rampant, unchecked by the sort of parents who encourage their offspring to "express themselves": little Tarquin and Henrietta shouting in the solemn remains about how boring the whole thing was, a thought internally echoed by the parents pretending to find the bits of cup and axe handles fascinating insights into their ancestors. Exhausted at the steep walk into the museum, and the oppressive heat inside, I tried to focus my concentration on the fragments, honing in on a pestle and mortar, reading the info as holy scripture, as the kids leapt and screamed around. I faked interest in a desperate attempt to redeem the £10 entry charge, taking opportunities to accidentally slap the little darlings in the head as I walked past. In the canteen, I sat beside a wailing baby, a bored brother and sister making outrageous attempts to disgust each other, and parents snapping in embarrassment at their shenanigans. I wolfed down the lukewarm coffee and shortbread, £5 each. Behind the museum, a beautiful view of the Atlantic, impossible to appreciate for the dozens of snappers and oohers and children.

I went home. I made the familiar decision that writers take when confronted with the humdrumness of real human beings: to abandon drawing inspiration from the locals and invent outlandish unbelievable characters who speak in overly contrived literary language. I opened the novel with a piece of dialogue making this clear, and in the character of

Isobel Bartmel, torpedoed realistic speech into the Atlantic. The opening five chapters led to the councillors and marketers making frantic phone calls to me. The councillor:

"I know, there are no 'believable' characters . . . no one speaks like people in novels. But readers want an approximation of how people speak. They can't stand characters that defy every standard human mode of speech. No one talks in these cute little puns and neologisms that you have this Isobel speaking in. You must think about the wider readership!"

"Have you read Virginia Woolf's *Flush*?"

"We can't sell a novel about a word-drunk librarian and an acidic elitist critic to the Scottish masses."

"I can't understand word one of this."

"We don't deal with authors who intend to spend their careers in small-press obscurity. Please write more accessible phrases and more relatable characters and more likeable situations and loveable words in general."

26

THE WEDDING happened a week later. Marcus spent his remaining time as a single man in the bedroom forcing himself to read *Bel-Ami* and *Fanny Hill* and *The Castle* and *London Fields* before the service while Isobel set up the "alternative" rituals that were to be performed at the service. He read twelve pages of each before Isobel was shouting at him to sling on his tux and mount the tandem. Once on the tandem, the couple pedalled church-wards and, at Isobel's insistence, up the aisle towards the vicar. The small congregation rose, performed a military salute, and sat on their whoopee cushions: twenty-seven simultaneous farts followed. The vicar said: "Hello, I am a church man. I hereby process your order to marry, and offer a complimentary shoehorn as a token of my depreciation." Isobel took the shoehorn and kissed the vicar on the cheek. The vicar said: "God says everything is groovy with this one. Marcus, you must promise to be an attentive father and husband to Isobel's child and Isobel respectively, and Isobel, you can continue to rock the island with your spangle and sass. Everyone rise to sing hymn number forty-four, 'High Five (Rock the Catskills)' by Beck." Marcus, too amazed to negotiate the terms of the marriage with the vicar, or to insert a reading-time clause into the verbal contract, found himself back on the tandem pedalling down the aisle, out the doors, zooming down the ramp and up into the back of a truck, crashing into a jacuzzi as the truck sped off to Kirkwall port. Isobel instigated ferocious intercourse in the bubbling water, sucking the breath from Marcus until his seed had been deported into her ovum and she could pretend this was the seminal inseminal moment that led to her gravidation. The truck arrived at the port, where the soaking couple boarded a private speedboat to Dishes (in Stronsay), and walked in the sunshine towards a private cottage, where after separate showers and a cheese sandwich, the honeymoon commenced.

On a coastal walk she said: "Now we're married, Marcus, I hope we can whittle a character for you. You have been patient in putting up with the zaniness I impose on a daily basis, and I realise your initial mission has been interrupted. So here are the options. You can appear with me in public at various times and adopt a similar zaniness, and become known on the island as a male version of me. Or, you can hang back and let me take centre stage, and become known as the long-suffering hubbie of that batshit bint Isobel. Either way, I will make sure you have enough time to read every day, provided you care for the kid at home, perform your husbandly duties with me in the sack, visit my parents, and attend those public things I mentioned. I would recommend the first option as being more exciting and likely to make our union more harmonious for however long we can make it last without killing each other."

"I suppose I could feign some zaniness if I had the time to read *The Ragged-Trousered Philanthropists*," Marcus said.

"You will have to work on your phrasing. I spent time cultivating a kind of kook in the cadences of my sentii. You can carve out a similar style of saying . . . I use alliteration by the ounce and a little rhythmic bounce. You could speak in short syllables, or long ones, or modulate your tone at random moments. Ponder on."

27

THE HONEYMOON: an awkward coastal walk around Stronsay attempting to find areas of mutual interest; a speedboat ride around the island resulting in a collision with a rock and a frantic swim back to land; a series of evenings spent watching Isobel's favourite Louis Malle films, from *Zazie dans le Métro* to *My Dinner with Andre*; Marcus's slow dawning that to conduct the rest of his life in so scenic a vista would not be perpetual torture, and that since siring a sprog with Sandra Acer was the paradise lost to him forever, raising one with this amiable wacko was not a foul alternative; Isobel's concern that Marcus might not compliment her character, and that she might lose standing on the island and take up swizzle-chugging to cope with the long nights of unfabulousness and screw up her kid's life; the continual struggle for a 4G signal in the Dishes cottage; the nights of increasingly tame sex on the creaky bed after the alcohol store had begun to dwindle; the unspoken mutual sense that the marriage might have been a mistake but there was nothing left to do except knuckle down and have a decent stab; the contrived optimism on the final day listening to Jesus and Mary Chain's *Psychocandy* and cleaning up the cottage; the pregnancy test produced on the final day, announcing the foetus with a dramatic flourish that Marcus sensed to be fake, but knowing the false enthusiasm he would have to stir up for the rest of his life, reacted to with exaggerated amazement; the successful return to Kirkwall where Isobel's parents met them off the speedboat and invited them to sit in their mobile home for five hours; their return to Isobel's home to conduct their lives with whatever pleasant or unpleasant outcomes emerged.

On Reading

Bore on a Train

"NOW A MINIM on the perils of train reading. Here is a short para-bore on reading Nicholson Baker's *The Mezzanine*," I said to the workshop. "Whenever I board a train I look for the seat farthest from other passengers as possible. To read, I need silence, or near silence—I need at least five or six seats distance. Finding the right seat is an exact science. One night, coming home from a concert, I enter the car and there are people spread at an infuriating equidistance apart, almost positioned on purpose at four-seat spaces to upset the four-to-six space rule. I walk past the menacing night-people, who are all potential murders and rapists until proven otherwise, and locate a seat in the left row between two solo passengers, with a space of about three seats in front and two seats behind and another man two seats ahead in the right row. A trio of women conduct a conversation up ahead, their voices muted at first but rising from time to time, competing with the rattle of the moving train. This is the strongest threat to an undisturbed reading of Baker. *The Mezzanine* requires concentration and is not train-fodder. The protagonist discusses the exaggerated minutiae of certain trivial aspects of his life, from shoelaces to escalator etiquette, to the value of paper towels over hand driers, each topic accumulating an absurd level of detail with laughter as the release. I read for a few moments and a loud titter interrupts. These are not the sober revellers I had assumed in that micro-second of noticing. These women are about to embark on a drunken confab punctuated with shrieks and whoops. I fight. I keep reading. I am unable to mute their drivel about some bloke being a dick and someone needing to phone someone and tell him something about being a dick or something because he shouldn't have said that, whoever he is, this traitorous dick. There are further dilemmas. I am short-sighted with a slight squint, and the lights on Scotrail trains are diffuse and dim. Reading the footnotes becomes a chore for me, trying to follow these complex tangents in the Granta edition's petite font under appalling lights, and the darkness outside offers no help. I can't bring the book right up close, as this can affect my long-range vision. If I am focusing on focusing my eyes, I'll stop focusing my brain—reading and not taking in the words. I wait until the women leave. At the next stop, the paranoia that a lunatic has boarded the train and wants to kill me becomes so intense, I have to look up and make a quick assessment of the new passenger, check his psycho credentials. If he sits behind me, which he does, I will have to keep one hand on my possessions, in case he should slide a hand through the half-inch seat space and steal my valuables. I am alone in the train with a psycho behind me. Paranoia increases as I contemplate the horrors of being robbed or stabbed. I picture a pocket knife being poked into my ribs, a wire being stretched across my neck. There's no point reading now, not with death on the cards. I become dour, thinking about other problems—financial, personal, familial—making each problem into something huge and insurmountable, until I can't stand to even hold the book, so depressed and self-involved have I become in those four minutes. I have read almost half a page." I waited for a hum of approval. No hum. "I hope this illustrates the perils of train reading. Find the quietest car. If boisterous sorts enter: move to another car. If there's too much bustle: park the reading until home. You don't want to miss a word."

28

ELEVEN MONTHS later, Marcus hadn't completed *The Ragged-Trousered Philanthropists*. He had started the book upon returning to Kirkwall, nailing 96 pages over two days, then Isobel held a soirée for her friends, and Marcus fell with ease into his role as the zany husband. He made this speech: "When I met Isobel, it was love at first fright. She terrified the pantaloons off me! I hid from her in the sci-fi section, but she cornered me square in the Philip K. Dicks. I told her I was looking for a space opera with lasers, and she produced *Quasar Lovin'* by Frink Elders, a romantic romp on board the Apollo 39. From there, we mounted our own space opera with lasers and lovin', our first date at the observatory, looking up at the stars where we were to live for two rapturous months of laughin' and lovin'. I first came here to read Dr. Peter Boxall's list of 1001 books. I confess I came here to sit in a cottage reading this chump's favourites, but once Isobel arrived and blasted me into outer space, I came to realise that life is nowhere to be lived in books. At the end of all that reading, I would have done less living than one tumultuous day out in Thurso. I focused instead on becoming fabulous. I am pleased to see you all here, and I hope you will wish us well in our connubial daze. To us!"

THE DEATH OF
THE READER

I

Far from becoming fabulous, Marcus instead embraced ordinariness. Isobel had found the wedding speech suspect—a prelude to the toxic embrace of a bookless existence—and made sure her man met his reading quotient. To appease her, Marcus swotted plot summaries on Wikipedia and reworked the descriptions over evening dinner, a practice that fooled her for two weeks, until she realised his readings were at best incompetent, at worst, cribbed from a fourth-former's half-arsed assignment, and that the words coming from his mouth had that particular funk of stilted insincerity common to the otiose plagiarist.

"Your reading of *Tess of the d'Urbervilles* as a proto-feminist text reeks of the mundane," she said over a roast dinner.

"Alas," Marcus said, sopping a sprout in a puddle of Bisto and nibbling round its damp circumference, "if I was able to summon up an original response to that perennial I would own a fleet of Bentleys."

"Hmm. I wonder what sparked this surge of interest in the canon. To read a classic is to lounge on the hammock of precooked interpretations, free from the onerous task of constructing one's own chesterfield of new meanings."

"Yes," Marcus said, twirling mash round his fork like a child caressing the mane of a plastic troll. "However, you have to read the fogies. Hardy's hardiness cannot be ignored. Millions feast on his pastoral miseries still."

"True. Hey, when you're finished, I have a read for you. *Trawl* by B.S. Johnson. I plan to read the novel this week. Perhaps we can engage in a tête-à-text après? B.S. was a bruiser with the brass balls to blurb Beckett without permission. His bullheadedness brought brainy books to blokes on the omnibus."

"Really?"

"Nup. But he's the closest thing we have to a man-on-the-street avant-gardener."

"Interesting."

"You will partake?"

"No. Sounds like BS to me."

"Ooft."

2

HIS MORNINGS were spent in an island-wide stride. He strode to open his mind to the pleasures of automaton living and to silence the carping Marcuses telling him to keep reading and realise his ridiculous dream. He peered into windows to observe automaton living at its apogee: men and women making cups of tea and parking their bottoms on the sofa to peer at nitwits in studios shouting at each other. He found this a tolerable preoccupation provided the mornings and afternoons were punctuated with biscuits. Hour-long programmes about antiques or crocheting could be tolerated with two coffees and half a pack of chocolate nibbles, after which information about the engravings on a bronze lamp led to a sugar-swooned sensation of interest that kept him high until *Countdown*. In the two hours before Isobel returned home, he would acquaint himself with the Wikipedia summation of whatever novel he was pretending to read for the sake of remaining in Isobel's nest. During the ad breaks, he contemplated the sweet surrender of ordinariness: the freedom at losing the fight to appear unique in a world where unique people roamed the streets in their hordes, screaming their individualities into megaphones, flaunting their brilliance and urging others to showcase their own qualities, merging into one blob of amazingness indistinguishable from the next blob of amazingness. Release came from accepting one's own failure to prove beyond all reasonable doubt that you were somehow different from the next person, that in fact you were the same as the next person, or even better, a pale imitation of everyone else, no little than a chalk outline of a human being.

On Writing

The Marketers Descend

A s I BEGAN chapter fifteen, as I wrote the sentence panning Iain Banks's first novel, as I sipped from a mug of hot chocolate tittering at the pathetic pleasure I had taken in spitting at a dead man's lauded first novel (the first novel I wrote, which I consider to eclipse Banks's, received no such adoration), I heard a knocking at the front door. Expecting this to be the postman with some books (I could order books online easily, with no extra P&P for island delivery), I was surprised to see the the two marketers who had been emailing me with velocitous snark for two months stood in catalogue-casual wear holding a hamper of cheese and wine.

"A peace offering!" the man one said.

Unshaven and pantless, clad in a morning robe, I accepted the offering with robotic bemusement and invited them to sit on chairs. I slung on a tee and slacks and boiled the kettle. Martha and Agnus were their names, and their couch-sitting was some of the sm(n)uggest I had witnessed: at ease on the couch at once, their arms in sprawl over the rest, exuding an air of ownership.

"What's happening with the novel?" Martha asked.

"Did you receive our latest notes?" Agnus asked.

"Has the kookiness been downtoned?" Martha asked.

"No, no, and I am about to write a sex scene between Isobel and Marcus. I received a note about spicing up the story, like E.L. James. Remember note #135, 'consensual sadomasochism is a hot product,' well. I might write a whipping scene."

"In straightforward prose?" one of them asked.

"More tea?" I dodged.

As I fingered on my phone the latest emails, I uncropped a conversation into which I had been accidentally CC'ed. The councillors were in a panic—it was too late to transfer the cash to another writer. Various ideas had been suggested to displace me: to set up a fake twitter account from my IP spouting racist views; to scour my past publications for evidence of an unhinged mind; to quiz ex-lovers on embarrassing incidents with which I could be blackmailed; to commission a ghostwritten book on the side, and stick my name on the cover when publication time came around; to have me killed. The councillors needn't have been so obsessed: no one, except the other writers passed over for the prize, cared about "New Writer" awards. One name was the same as another to an indifferent reading public. Council-approved books were about their topics and issues. The most aggressive council-backed authors fought to keep themselves around on the scene until reviewers started using phrases like "old favourite" or "reliable hand," and their place in the established order was assured. The councillors had chosen to send the marketers up to "influence" the direction of the novel.

"Can we see what you're writing at the mo?" Agnus asked. I showed them the fifteenth chapter and awaited their irritating comments.

"How can one 'mid-dangle'?"

"More neolojizzing," Martha said.

"Ooft. Insulting one of the most popular Scottish novels of all time?"

"I am about to list some better Scottish novels," I added.

"This isn't contractually satisfactory," etc.

Moving themselves into the spare room, a week of tacit seductions began. Noticing their patronising corporate tack had no impact, on the second day, Operation Best Mates began. An afternoon of treats was planned for me pending the morning's write: a trip to a neolithic brick museum containing a lump of rampart from an early cathedral; a round of bowls with the nonagenarians at the green; a slap-up three-course at the priciest tourist bistro; a late-night boogie with the teenagers at the noise-restricted nightclub next to a retirement home. The marketers had read *Morvern Callar*, a novel in which two publishing twats attempt to seduce the female halfwit protagonist cribbing her dead boyfriend's success, and thought I would find these egregious activities a whirlwind treat. I complained about the tedium of the museum, the heart attacks interrupting play on the green, the ludicrousness of £25 for a burger and chips, and the hushed gyrations to Orbital at the club. My hope was this incessant whining would cause them to flee in disgust.

Not so.

3

Eight months into her bumpitude, Isobel arrived on Raine Upright's slabs in a morose frump. Her husband had imprinted himself into her purple-cerise Loafer Supreme with the frightful intention of embracing fatherhood when the foetus formed. Raine had written nine sentences since twelve o'clock and was limping through a tenth when the bell sounded. His latest collection, *Cannoning the Canon*, performed seppuku on the familiar names, from Austen to Madox Ford to Shelley to Zola. She required an open ear into which to pour her moans and Marcusses. Raine required an excuse to leave the cursor winking within another asinine squelcher at the expense of his heroes and heroines. In her flesh-coloured tank top baring the slogan *Napster is Dead*, unborn load in evidence, she entered the premises: upon entrance, Raine served a half-pint of Diet Pepsi and a bowl of pretzels.

"To recap," Raine said after six minutes of Isobellyache, "the situation. This chump cornered into servitude, i.e. the husband, has been husbanned from not-reading novels. Having lapsed into the routine of a workless shiftless prole, fending off complaints with the cherubic rubric of pending paternity, you find this behaviour vexing. Your two conditions—constant reading and tip-top fathering—are not being met. His preparing for the latter and spurning the former is boiling up boke in your bowels."

"I've missed your circumshotlocutions. Your circumloejaculations. Yes, Raine. In other words: the weasel promised to read novels. Why, when he moved here to swallow Boxall's poxy swill, has the impulse vanished?"

"I can explain this phenomenonandonandon. You see, the Great Schott went north to reassert the manhood that a fed-up femme had taken in her fat palms and scrunched into an ickle ball. He schemed a scheme to blow his ickle balls back to burgeoning *ballissimo*. Like that time we had a fling. You fed me romantic notions like so much beluga caviar and within two weeks had me on my knees nibbling on rotten tripe. Once Marcus scored himself a foxy beanpole librarian for a wife, those balls reballooned."

"Beanpole no more," Isobel said, referring to the Isobelly, "and foxy, eh? The fling we had was a nano-a-nano mano-a-womano. Have you read *Trawl*, by the who, by B.S. Johnson, by the way?"

"Yes. A harrowing column of stomach-churning recall."

"You have a solution for this Marcussedness?"

"You could cripple his manhood again. Spend the night recapping those emasculating lies once murmured into my ear on this very divan."

"So restore your manhood and smash Marco's?"

"Equipoison us."

Isobel accepted the chance to unman her man with this man under the sheets. Having not slept with Raine for a pleasant spell, she forgot the foibles: his insistence on being blindfolded to mentally interpose Muriel Spark into the bed in place of the real woman; his insistence on retaining his socks to create additional friction between the sheets and his feet; his insistence on climbing on top and refusal to negotiate his member into the pertinent area; his insistence on reciting stanzas from Seamus Heaney towards climax. Raine's beerbelly, bumping up against the Isabelly, led to a bellycose collision—bellies too close to be cosy—and a necessary realigning of naughties in their nighties. Isobel's reverse cowgirling led to a swift comeuppance, Raine at his peak: "The hillside blushed, soaked in our broken wave!", and an even swifter comedownance with Isobel leaping back into her clothes. She raided the fridge for fizz and fizzed on the divan in a certain repulsed nostalgia. "Better to bonk a bookworm than bonk a bookless worm," she said to an M.C. Escher print.

4

ATTENTION, ORKNEY! WE ARE THE PEOPLE IN GREY. WE . . .

NO, READ *THAT* BIT . . .

THIS BIT?

YES, DAMMIT.

WE ARE TAKING OVER. FOR TOO LONG WE HAVE BEEN CAST ASIDE LIKE SLABS OF MOULDY CAMEMBERT OR AN UNWANTED SAUSAGE POKED AROUND THE PLATE OF A NINE-YEAR-OLD GIRL. AS OF TODAY, WE WILL REPLACE THE COUNCIL AS RULERS OF THE ISLAND—

REPLACE THE *GOVERNMENT*.

YES, WE WILL REPLACE THE GOVERNMENT. USING WEAPONS PURCHASED FROM THE DARK NET FROM NORWEGIAN SMUGGLERS—YES, NORWEGIANS CAN BE EVIL TOO—WE WILL FORCE YOU ALL TO OBEY. AS YOU LISTEN TO THIS, YOUR LANDLINES, MOBILES, AND INTERNET CONNECTIONS HAVE ALL BEEN STOPPED, GIVING YOU NO MEANS OF COMMUNICATING WITH THE MAINLAND. THE NEW REGIME WILL BEGIN SHORTLY. ALL FERRIES AND BOATS TO THE MAINLAND HAVE BEEN CANCELLED. ESCAPE IS IMPROBABLE. PLEASE RETURN TO YOUR HOMES AND AWAIT FURTHER INSTRUCTION. FOR THOSE NOT IN KIRKWALL, PLEASE TUNE YOUR RADIOS TO 104.40 FM TO HEAR THESE COMMANDS.

BUT THEY WON'T . . .

WHAT?

NOTHING, STOP TALKING NOW.

WHAT DO I PRESS?

THAT ONE.

THIS ONE?

OH, FOR FU—

5

FOR HALF a decade, the marginalised colourless minorities had been sitting in bars necking swizzles to keep the colorful characters convinced that their traits were the most significant, and that their failure to be interesting made them unique. At closing time, the minorities mobilised in the house of Brian Moxhatts, a former turpentine salesman turned clueless wifeless childless hopeless useless man, to plan their coup over those with the wit or spirit enough to transcend the barren nightmare of their surroundings. Having little imagination, the men chose to use violence to overthrow the citizenry, and took their time learning the intricacies of ordering weapons online without the police arriving at their doors in under two minutes. Moxhatts had curdled into hate over his long time as a lessful man and led the People in Grey (PiG) to their current positions: stood at each compass point of Kirkwall holding machine guns, preventing people from fleeing and rounding them into the town hall.

At the town hall, half the population assembled to listen to their new leaders. Brian Moxhatts was a pallid lank with the awkward poise of a shoegazing bassist and, in his brown cardigan and even browner slacks, loomed over the lectern to utter: "The reign of the colorful characters is over. We are the People in Grey, and we are taking back the island. Our plans involve a series of calculated revenges to occur in the mornings at the coast at Tankerness. The first of these is a series of floggings. Please report to Francis Grunge's house at 8.15am tomorrow for the first of these. Our PiG agents will round up those who fail to report and an additional penalty of nine smacks of the birch rod will be included for this insolence. We will announce our other intentions later. In the meantime, please return to your houses." The one weapon available to the island's "characters"—imagination and pluck and cleverness—was ineffective when a machine gun was pointed at them.

Mild muttering followed as people returned to their homes.

On Reading

System for Proper Appreciation

"LISTEN, READERS! You sail through these sentences and paragraphs. All that effort us writers put in to have a handful of strangers looking at our words for two or three days, and you place them aside for words more palatable to your tastes. Sure, we might 'connect' with you, you anonymous swine, we might 'move' you, or make you titter, but do we really care if one of our sentences takes you to higher plane of existence, or binds you to us for a flickering moment, when you will 'forget' to read our next book, or express 'disappointment' at its failure to replicate the exact experience you had reading the last, or any other of your incalculable readerly neuroses that you are free to exercise, and that we must tolerate without ever expressing our true feelings, i.e. that we think you are a batch of irritating fuckwits with no proper method for appreciating and respecting authors," I said. The workshop stared at me like a beaver regarding a lapsed arch. "I can offer an example. The first Martin Amis work I read was the story collection *Heavy Water*. The book had no particular impact on me, so I placed Amis on the backburner for a while. A few years later, I thought I might attempt a novel, so I picked up *Money*, and was impressed. Not so impressed that I felt I must attack the oeuvre with a violent passion (as in the cases of Gilbert Sorrentino, Ali Smith, Christine Brooke-Rose, and others), but enough to spur me on to continue exploring his works. I read *Experience* next and a few months later *London Fields*. I loved them. I became a devoted fan and anticipated reading the rest of his works. Sadly, the next novel I read was *Other People*, which was so terrible I couldn't believe the same author's name was on the cover. Now, some readers at this point would have wiped Amis from their future reading lists forever. I have an airtight system for dealing with these sorts of bumps. I had read two Amises I considered not bad, two I loved, and one I loathed. Since the balance was more on the favourable side, I owed Amis another read. If this next read proved terrible, this would create more of a love-to-hate equilibrium (in fact, two hates, two so-sos, two loves), and the next book I would read would decide whether I continued reading Amis or not. To explain in simpler terms. I read one book by an author I love. The next I read I loathe. This means the next (third) novel has to impress to keep me reading the oeuvre. If the next (third) novel is so-so, I allow myself the freedom to discriminate based on the feelings of affection I had for the novel I loved. If I loved that novel so much that I felt that the author deserved a fourth chance, I would read another. If this fourth read was so-so, I would stop reading that author. If it was amazing, I would continue. This process of weighing continues, so if I read the fifth novel and loathed it, I might again consider offering another chance, recalling the two I loved. Two in the hate camp, however, makes this a difficult decision. Fortunately, this is a rare occurrence, as an author tends to click over the first few books or not. I chose Amis as someone who has divided me from book to book. To return to Martin. I offered him another chance after the horror of *Other People*, and read *The Information*. This became one of my favourite books. I lavished heaps of praise on the acerbic satire of the writer's life, and felt confident about reading another Amis. I picked up *House of Meetings* and had a rotten reading experience. At this point, the author's inconsistency maddened me, so I left him alone for awhile, choosing the safer option of his non-fiction next time. I read with happiness *The Moronic Inferno*. Dipping a toe into the fiction, I read the so-so *Night Train*. Then later, after a long hiatus, the non-fiction *Visiting Mrs. Nabokov*. A leap into recent Amis with *The Zone of Interest* left me impressed. However, I still feel an apprehension whenever I have an urge to read another Amis novel. The odds are in Amis's favour, however, so I owe him my readerly fidelity, recalling the peaks of *London Fields*, *Experience*, and *The Information*. You should adopt this system."

6

IT WAS ISOBEL'S turn to bend over and receive the birch rod. Her optometrist Oliver Putschmann was the man wielding the unbound twigs. Upon seeing Oliver, she opened up her arms wide for her usual vibrant hug. He shrank back lest the other flogging officers spotted him being familiar with a "character."

"I can't, Isobel," he said.

"Of course. I have to say, Ollie, I am surprised to see you cavorting with these cracked nobodaddies. You always struck me as a man with a passion for righting the retinae," she said.

"I am. Outside the office I am bland."

"Shame. All right, Ollie, let me have six of your worst. I can't bend over that much due to the unborn child thing."

"Look . . . I'm not flogging a pregnant woman. I'll pretend to flog you, and you make a moaning sound."

"Ollie, you're such a sweetnips. Take it away, then." Isobel bent over and stared out over Hangie Bay at the shimmering waters. It was a beautiful morning to be pretend-flogged. "Ouch!" she said, followed by: "Ouch! Ouch! Ouch! Ouch! Ouch! Ollie, you beast!" and "Ouch! Ouch! Ouch! Ouch! Ouch!"

"That's enough."

"Thanks, Ollie."

Forty lines of five hundred people formed. Each received their flogging swiftly, the whole procedure lasting an hour. Hank Righteous, a former used car salesman, channelled his indignation at the closure of Rover through hard and merciless thwacks across Marcus's bottom. Iain Grousel, a retired Modern Studies teacher, relished in hurting the cheeks of Raine Upright, the two having come to blows over the Iraq War and the later novels of Rosalind Belben. "This—oww!—does not mean—oww!—you have won our long-standing feud. Oww! *The Limit* is a far more interesting novel—oww!—than *Our Horses in Egypt* and you'd—oww!—have to be an idiot to believe—oww!—otherwise," Raine said bent over staring out at the shimmering waters and tempting cliff-faces.

7

THE PiG TRIED to split the populace into three camps: Scholars, Traders, and Prancers. Scholars were those who held positions that involved reading or brainpower; Traders those in manual occupations; and Prancers those who showed too much vim and brio regardless of their status. These categories proved inadequate, as there were people who fit into two or three, such as George Cameroon: an eccentric man who showed scholar-like levels of knowledge about the Boer War, and worked as a mechanic. Vivian Horfield was a professor at the Open University prone to parading up Kirkwall high street in peacock feathers. Archie Concave had never worked in his life and sang the hits of George Michael while riding a tricycle up and down the island. Disputes ensued. The PiG officers quizzed people on the spot. "Do you prance like Mr Thing?" one asked a deaf OAP. "Do you consider yourself hip-to-the-groove?" one asked a sweet nurse. "Is there a high percentage of swank in your gait?" one asked a squat Irishman. "Does the sun emanate from your posterior?" one asked a shy toddler. Baffled citizens replied in the negative, positive, and negative again, unsure which camp of the three would prove the most punitive. Maud Granger replied to the accusation of blingitude: "No, this necklace is an homage to Alan Sillitoe!" and was hurled into the Prancer camp. David Klinkowitz was berated for his tattoo of The Kinks—"a working-class band!"—and flung into the Prancer camp. As Isobel was being interrogated about her "fanciful manner of expression," her waters broke. The PiG took this as a pathetic attempt to free herself from the Prancer camp and hurled her towards the Prancer camp. Raine noticed this rough handling and leapt on the PiG, wrestling with him towards the cliff-face, where the PiG rolled over the side to his end and Raine managed to latch on to a convenient rock. Pandemonium ensued. Distraught PiG began firing into the air, causing people to stampede. Paul Verveson shouted: "This is the end of me!" and leapt up and down on the spot until a PiG officer punched him. People fled back towards the road. Others remained to fight. Marcus nudged through the thicket of bellicose PiG and manic normals to locate a doctor. The first shot was fired. Paul Thimblewhill had shouted: "Death to the PiG!" and was shot in the head. Bettie Verso shouted: "Please, are we barbarians?" and was shot in the chest. Marcus snatched Dr. Craig Woodruff after he had finished urinating on a PiG pinned to the grass. Dragging Isobel to a safe location (behind the rock that had saved Raine), Marcus helped with the birth of his firstborn. Raine, recovering from his near-death moment, snatched a pistol from one of the slain PiG and kept attackers at bay by waving the thing in the air and making this sound: "Nooowaaaoooooaaaa!"

On Writing

The Marketers Abscond

A FTER YESTERDAY'S botched schmoozing, the marketers tried to perk me up with perkier perks.

"Publishing a market-ready novel comes with bonuses," Agnus said over his poached egg.

"What those be?" I asked over a boiled ditto.

"You like novels? We can send free review copies of—"

"—the sort of *farkatke* fogey-fodder the council endorses?" I eggter-jected.

"You like authors?" Martha asked over her scramble same, "we can introduce you to some of the best names—"

"—in the realm of *bobkes* books?"

"You want tips? Writing masterclasses from some of—"

"—the sloppiest *shmendriks* in the business?"

"You like parties and fun? You can meet some of—"

"—the booziest *shikers* in the room?"

"Are you Jewish?" Martha asked.

"I'm a *sheygets*, sweetie," I shyaid.

"So will you rewrite the novel?"

"You poor *shlemazl*."

The next day, sabotage was the strategy. I was prepared for their "accidental" attacks: Agnus spilled a beaker of Blue Nun over my lap-top, causing a meltup and shutdown. I had saved my documents on nine USBs. En route to the tech repair shop, Martha accidentally hurled my laptop off a cliff. I had a backup laptop under my bed. "You can use ours! And this template for the new MS!" Martha said. She opened up a half-written populist novel and nodded me on for completion. I inserted a USB and pasted the MS over the pre-written turd and resumed the sex scene in chapter fifteen. Martha winced as I wrote "seminal fluid shooting up Isobel's tubes," and searched the room for something to smash the USB. "There's the female audience gone," she said. "My books don't have a female audience," I replied. I returned from a bathroom break to find the USB hammered to smithers. (I had saved the writing so far to the one in my back pocket). "Sorry, my mallet slipped," Agnus said. He had brought a mallet.

"Right, this is *ongepatsht*. Stop smashing items I own. You two are eating up the eggs and messing up the main room. You think two advertising *nudniks* tried to sabotage Paul West or Jonathan Swift's novels?"

"Who's Paul West?"

"Who's Jonathan Swift?"

Having failed at matiness, bribery, and sabotage, seduction was the final step. Martha had made the decision that I would prefer to snack on Agnus's cock, so the large man and his little man appeared at midnight by the cupboard.

"You want?" he asked like a coy concubine.

"You out of the room now? Yes."

"Not interested?"

"Nope." He sent Martha in a negligee into the room. I weighed up the moral implications of sleeping with Martha that evening and refusing to write the horrendous novel in the morning. Her repugnance at sharing a room with me was large, so sharing orifices with me would induce an uneraseable trauma in her, which as a punishment for her remarkable career sacrifice was rather steep.

"Out," I said.

"What? You into dogs? Gerbils?"

"Ocelots. Beat it."

The marketers packed up. By daybreak the only trace of their presence was a few leftover eggs, a mallet, and a post-it reading "You will regret this."

8

THE BABY, a female, was born on the cliff edge and swaddled in Raine's coat. A four-mile detour around the scene of the skirmish followed with several stops for Isobel to collapse in the grass and colour the landscape with fucks. Back at Isobel's cottage, after a twelve-hour nap, she named the child Funkadelic.

"Funkawhat?" Marcus asked.

"You might find this choice curious, but in light of the recent PiG uprising, I need to make a gesture of resistance," Isobel explained. Funkadelic suckled on her left teat.

"Now isn't the time to rebel. These maniacs have killed. Peter Simpson from the chemist shot four people, among them sweet old Bettie Horsebottom from the Marie Curie Cancer Research shop!" Raine added. Marcus looked at Raine who looked at Isobel who looked at Marcus who looked at Isobel who looked at Raine who looked at Marcus who looked at Raine. This sequence of looks confirmed that Isobel was comfortable exposing her breasts before the two males and that the two males were uncomfortable sharing the sight of the exposed breasts, in spite of their mutual awareness of each having sucked them on separate occasions.

"If the PiG learn about that name, we risk a hilltop stabbing," Marcus said.

"Let me utter the following nouns, verbs, adjectives, adverbs, and prepositions: these piggies pose no peril to us *ci-deviants*. Chaps, we have here a case of the Outsider Tantrum. As a native, I am familiar with the menace of these mewls, the pull of these pules: when the cot rages the rot rises. To appease the losers and boozers: we let them into Klub Kool. We utter: You are a special species. You are a spectral specimen. We are nothing in comparison to the koolness and kookitude that emanates from your oh-so-amazing orifices," Isobel said. Raine made a face that said: "Complete arsecake."

"Complete arsecake. You stick to suckling. We'll make better words with our mouths that produce in those same words a solution. Right, Markie-pouch?"

"Yes," Marcus replied. He wanted to speak a sentence like that one, but at that moment his language was vanilla. "How about Claire?"

"How about Miss Blandface McBlandtits?" Isobel replied.

"I suggest: Rikki, Regine, Colette, Pandora, Fionnuala, Nadine," Raine said.

"I cannot calculate the precise proportion of puke I am making at the hideousness of those suggestions," Isobel said. She swapped teats and the two males looked toward the blinds and the carpet respectively. "All right, coyo boyos. Stop behaving like third-form squeamers around the milking process. Please accept the presence of suckling as a necessary reality in your lives. Consequently, this nipper is causing me untold agony with its nipping lips on my nipping nips." The men said nothing.

"Please reconsider Funkadelic," they said.

"Please change little Funky's nappy," Isobel said. "I must rest."

9

THE TANKERNESS massacre, where ten civilians had bullets wedged in their bodies and five PiG were mauled beyond repair, forced the terrorists to strengthen their resolve. The PiG, in teams of two, went from bothy to bothy rounding up the escapees, taking them to the HQ of their respective camps. Isobel had spent an hour rocking Funkadelic to sleep, and as she collapsed in bed the PiG arrived at her door with a megaphone that said: "OPEN UP, YOU USELESS VORTEX OF HUMANITY. OPEN UP OR WE WILL SHOOT YOU IN THE GUTS, LIKE WE DID THOSE OTHERS!" Raine, sleeping on the couch, opened up to confront the two hostile agents: Holly Polish, receptionist at Mine Howe, and Gregor Volume, forklift operator for McDowell Operations. "Ssshhh!" he ssshhhed.

"YOU ARE TO COME WITH US TO—"

"Put the megaphone down," Holly said.

"Shut up, you nitwits. There's a newborn sleeping upstairs. Holly, is that thou? Surprised to see you PiGging it up with these oinkers. I always found your Mine Howe welcomes showcased the voom of your oral."

"Eh? You're that pretentious ponce who tried to chat me up with a Dickens quote, ain't you?"

"Yes. From *Little Dorrit*. 'While the flowers, pale and unreal in the moonlight, floated away upon the river; and thus do greater things that once were in our breasts, and near our hearts, flow from us to the eternal sea.' People overlook that later novel, but it's actually one of Chaz's most trenchant and moving epics." Holly responded to this ill-timed literary opinion with a violent tugging into the armiture of Gregor, a brawn with no brains who apehandled Raine into his Volvo S40. Isobel and Marcus were roused from their sleeps with prods. "Oi. Oi. Oi. Oi," Holly said, prodding. She snatched up Funkadelic, placed her into Isobel's arms, and prodded them into the Volvo in their jammies.

The trio were labelled Scholars and dropped into the public library, where the front and inside doors were manned with men and their machine guns and their bullets and their killing potential. "Fabulous! Back at work two days after giving birth! That's modern Britain for you!" Isobel said. One of the PiGs tittered and was slapped for tittering. "Titters outlawed too? You bunch are boo-hoo sad." About one hundred people filled the library, camped on the floor in unspeaking huddles. Isobel, Marcus, Raine, and Funkadelic sat below the classics shelf, outstaring the others who seemed to believe these latecomers were responsible for their encampment, and conveyed this suspicion with furtive stares that said: "You are the reason I might end up a corpse atop a stack of Stephen Kings."

On Reading

Abandonment

"THERE IS NOTHING WORSE, workshop," I said to the workshop, who were tweeting about how wretched I was, "than having to abandon a book. Let me sluice out some reasons. First, in the case of classics: these are books above blame. It is always your fault. Now, I am not speaking about the new Penguin Modern Classics edition of Nick Hornby's *Fever Pitch* or some other idiocy, I am speaking about the black classics, the white classics, the blue classics, the free ebook classics, the overpriced facsimile classics: in short, the classic Classics. You hate *The Decameron*? Fuck you. You struggled to 'slog through' *Middlemarch*? Fuck you. You had to abandon *A Tale of Two Cities* because your hectic work schedule made you lose track of the plot? Fuck you. You found *A Sentimental Education* too self-indulgent? Fuck you. You can't follow the Chaucerian English of Chaucer? Fuck you. You think Charlotte Brontë's *Shirley* is meandering and preachy? Correct. Sorry, I mean fuck you. You are always to blame. At some point in your reading life, all these books will make sense. Perhaps they won't. Either way, assaulting a Classic simply shows up your own failure as a reader. Forget it, fuckers." I was enjoying the liberty I had taken in calling the workshop fuckers. Frenzied tweeting followed. "It's all right. Everyone fails at a classic or two. I still haven't completed a successful reading of *Madame Bovary* or *War & Peace*. Now, when it comes to commonplace literary fiction, there are multiple hiccups here. I once had a solid rule: fifty pages was the absolute minimum before abandoning. For the novice reader, I would enforce this. You are more likely to be less tolerant and need to train yourself to condition your mind to the author's be-bop and jazz, even if it reads at first like bum-plop and jizz. After a few years of this, you will become an expert at detecting a talented prose wizard from a mediocre hack. It is the responsibility of every writer to make their material of moderate magic from sentence to sentence to fucking sentence. If their novel about Tyneside carpetbaggers is not bursting with vibrant language, or at least weaves a supreme style from page to page, then that author is worth binning. Beware the hacks who trade on emotional manipulation and clichés refarted ad nauseam through a new orifice. Later, you can read the first ten pages of a novel and probably make up your mind on that basis. Yes, having to abandon a novel is painful. It causes an immense anger, usually aimed towards the author, and then at oneself for failing to appreciate a book probably called 'dazzlingly inventive' by some fucker in the *Guardian*. Keep away from social media. The urge to pan a novel and publicly humiliate the author for wasting your time is immense, but in the long run, the best revenge is to say nothing and read superior works."

As Isobel suspected, the PiG had no agenda per se. Orders were walkie-talkied to the agents to perform "minor torments" on the captives. Holly Polish proved to be the most vengeful of the agents and improvised acts of annoyance. Her small head contained a crushed-up face that required surgical stretching: the lips being too close to the nose, almost to the level of a novice gurner, with wide Germanic eyes and a fringe too long for her short forehead, poking into her eyes and causing an excess of blinking. Her ire had risen over seven years womanning the Mine Howe entrance in the cold Portakabin on the site: handing tourists brochures to be stuffed in bags and binned at the hotel, pointing to the entrance and warning visitors to take care on the stairs, having to rescue fallen OAPs and shrieking claustrophobics, collecting the used condoms from upright subterranean humps, and spending long lonesome hours not reading as the manager had instructed her to sit in wait for the arrival of visitors. These factors, including no sex, no siblings, and no parents since the age of twelve, led to Holly forcing Isobel to balance four hardbacks on her head and walk along a chalk line on the carpet: the punishment for failure four hard thwacks across the rump with Nicola Barker's *Darkmans*.

Isobel performed this task with aplomb, to the chagrin of Holly, who was looking forward to taking her revenge on the time Isobel rattled off Mine Howe facts she hadn't memorised from the pamphlets. Raine's sense of balance, ravaged by excess swizzles, earned him four hard thwacks, in spite of the fact Raine in his drunken ebullience had been prepared to have sex with her, and Marcus lost Graham Rawle's *Woman's World* at the last step, earning him the same painful hurt from Holly, scrunching her face in a hideous scowl of hate, at near-orgasmic levels of sadistic pleasure at her actions. "That face is the boot that will be stamping on our futures for an indeterminate period of time," Isobel said, paraphrasing Orwell.

"More like that boot has a face that has been stamped on forever," Raine remarked, rubbing his rump.

Among Holly's further torments: making them read aloud passages from novels and flinging tacks at their faces during hesitations or mispronounced words; forcing them to make origami penises from the pages in their favourite books; having them read long plot-driven novels then tearing out the last ten pages; making them alphabetise a thousand books in neat piles then knocking the piles over; forcing them to read a Barbara Cartland novel in exchange for a sandwich; having them sequence a thousand books in the order of percentage ratings on Goodreads from lowest to highest; forcing them to stuff as many books down their clothes as possible and dance the Macarena; making them chase a cupcake on a novel attached to a rope around the room on their knees.

11

"I CAN'T LAST much longer," Marcus whined.

"Nix the whine. All we need to do is murder Holly Goshitely," Isobel said.

"Marcus, I have noticed an upsetting unrelish to read etched upon thine brow," Raine said.

"Waaaaa!" Funkadelic said.

"What?"

"You approach books with the expression of a supermodel sitting directly opposite a vomiting tramp."

"I have suffered a minor lapse."

"No, mon emu. I recognise that visage. It is the look of the curate shaking hands with his son, the homosexual pimp. It is the look of the prim heiress as she is limousined in error through Harlem. It is the look of the aesthete upon tuning in to ITV3. It is the look of the vegetarian as her boyfriend slices into a steak fillet. It is the look of the nurse as the alcoholic necks his smuggled hipflask of absinthe. It is the look of the museum curator as a frolicking child trips up and smashes the ancient pterodactyl skeleton. It is the look of the dentist at 4.59pm when her patient opens his mouth to twelve cankers. It is the—"

"*Aaaaahhhh.* How many more?" Isobel asked.

"Maaaaaa?" Funkadelic asked.

"Some. It is the look of the janitor as the children run in from the rugby pitch. It is the look of the husband as the wife telephones her demanding mother. It is the look of the businessman as the Dow Jones buckles in half. It is the look of the bubblegumade salesman as his product is rendered revolting. It is the look of the author as the organiser tells him only two people turned up to his reading. It is the look of the reader on turning the page to a block of text with no paragraph breaks. It is the look of the optician upon realising her customer is blind. It is the look of the hairdresser upon spotting lice. It is the—"

"Yes?"

"No more."

"Yaaaaaaaay!" it sounded like Funkadelic said.

"Your point?" Marcus asked.

"Your reading lust has cooled. You no longer have that wanton verbivoracity when we first met in The Swaddled Firkin. As I understand the terms of your marriage, you are supposed to read enthusiastically, satisfy your wife, and care for your baby, so I wonder, are you honouring your verbal?"

"You told Raine?" Marcus asked his wife.

"It's serious," his wife said to him. "You are on the Marcusp of disaster. You had no intention of nailing Boxall's 1001 post-marriage. Your experiences in cottage chaos have flattened your afflatus to flatus. At the beginning I took rapidly to your Comstockian musk. You would not so much as sniff at George now. I feel ill-at-ease with a bookless boy, so I'm afraid I will be your wife in name only until the reading rebegins," Isobel said.

Marcus couldn't challenge the fact. In traducing literature in favour of husbandry, fatherhood, and normality, he found himself on the outset of a nervous breakdown of which he was unaware. At the moment, he held Funkadelic and showered the tot in loving utterances, cradling the creation with happiness, and even harboured ambitions to snuggle his wife in a loving manner with the tot sleeping across their bellies as the evening sun waned on their beautiful realities. And at the moment, this was a prospect he believed possible, once the PiG returned to their homes and ended the silliness.

"Also, I am having sex with Raine," she said. Raine stared up at the Dickenses.

"Oh," Marcus said. The prospect he believed a second ago seemed a fraction less probable to him now.

12

"YES, MUM, the baby is healthy and happy."
(Can't stop wailing when in Isobel's clutches).

"Still considering our options for the name. We have a few ideas."

(The child is named Funkadelic).

"Yes, Alison is a nice name. Mmm . . . Bonnie, Wendy, Henrietta, Maxine. Good suggestions."

(The child is named Funkadelic).

"We're fine. A little exhausted."

(From being tortured repeatedly for the last two days).

"Yes, the first week is proving the hardest. Isobel is shattered."

(The first week being tortured and raising the baby in a public library is proving the hardest).

"Yes, we're very happy all the same."

(About to divorce).

"No, I sold the cottage. Living with Isobel."

(Soon to be homeless when she kicks me out for not having read the complete works of Orwell).

"Yes, we will visit soon."

(If we are not shot in the head first).

"Can you hear me?"

(Probably not, since this is an imaginary conversation, the phone lines having been cut off).

"Sending our love."

(You will probably never see me again).

On Writing

Andrew Drizzwell

NEXT TO AMBUSH my peace was the poet Andrew Drizzwell, author of *Boat Atop the Boat* and *Rain After the Rain*, poems from which were collected in the *New Scottish Review*, *The Best New Scottish Verse*, *McLiterature: 50 Tartan Poems*, *Saltire's Song: Ten New Poets*, *New Writing Scotland 978*, and *The Skinny's Guide to Cool Shit We Like in 2016*. Ever since publishing a poem ("A Grain of Rice") in the *Edinburgh Review*, Andrew had taken on the serious contemplative air of the professional poet (before then he was like all other poets: confused, addicted to psychotropic substances, and in an abusive relationship with a barmaid). He entered my flat like a nonchalant superior, allowing his coat to be taken and a decaf to be offered, and cracked his knuckles in preparation for the swift conversion into "serious" writer he was about to perform on me. Pleasantries and coffees passed and we:

"Take this poem 'Ladies in Portraiture' I wrote, for example," Andrew forexampled. "I describe how the Great Painters arranged their models for some of the most famous portraits. I mention some of their names and the names of the sitters, capturing some of the details of their arrangements that caught my eye, and I throw in an Italian phrase to show the reader my intellectual pedigree. I actually went to the gallery, made notes on the paintings, and went home and wrote the poem. The word 'loved' is in the final line to lend the poem Emotional Resonance. Here, I have a copy of the poem in my chap—"

"No thanks."

"You can read it later. No rush. So I read the first fifteen chapters. I think the problem is there are no recognisable human interactions between your characters, who are by and large vehicles for your fondness for wordplay. Now, there's a place for this sort of thing. Some of the small presses put out tremendous novels for a limited readership.

However, since this Council-Backed Novel is intended to reach a Large Audience, I think there has to be some sandblasting of the indulgences," he said with his active mouth.

"You came here to repeat verbatim the 4,480 emails?"

"Not at all, mate. Look, there's a quote from Joy Williams I like to roll out on such occasions."

"Oh God."

"She says in her magnificent novel *The Changeling*, 'You must stop worrying about why things happen and wonder what they mean when they do.' Think about this in relation to our response to your new draft."

"What has happened is five desperate council stooges have been hoodwinked into publishing a decent fucking novel for a change, and you're flailing in panic because the media will pan the novel and you will look incompetent."

"You're an unpleasant chap."

"No. What is unpleasant, chap, is attempting to smother another writer's creativity by forcing him to write about Big Themes, Universal Emotions, Moving Moments, Life's Large Questions, Love & Death & Love & Love, when I want to write about a librarian who speaks in fast-paced comic babble, a bampot based on the author, and a critic who is the manifestation of all the author's shameless elitist interests."

"Elitist. Exactly."

"Look. I understand the pandering. People can't be trusted to read the right things. People will swallow whatever popular pap is thrown at their throats. We've long ago hit the Marianas Trench of bestswelling crumminess. A book of Kim Kardashian's bowel movements will sell seven billion copies while a new unearthed masterpiece from Thomas Bernhard will sell less than the population of Buford, Wyoming. Great Literature is an arthritic pensioner en route for an ice-caked hill. Great Literature is a messerschmitt in tailspin. Great Literature is an antique vase in the hands of a raging narcoleptic. Great Literature is a toilet roll placed before a manic kitten. Great Literature is a lost toddler in the path of a rampaging bull. Great Literature is a pneumonic man dumped in the arctic tundra. Great Literature is an obese child's lot upon being trapped in an organic veg shop. Great Literature is the likelihood of a swift passage through the town on a marathon day. Great Literature is a friendship struck up on the *Titanic*. Great Literature is a new single from REM. Great Literature is the likelihood of a writer obsessed with lists being published by Penguin. Great Literature is a sputum-heavy sneeze on a first date. Great Literature is a man wearing a 'Gay & Proud' t-shirt in Murmansk. Great Literature is a mother's face upon receiving Swans' *Soundtracks for the Blind* for Xmas. Great Literature is the second week after a new leader's election. Great Literature is an unguarded nutsack in a chimp's cage. Great Literature is a male black widow spider's post-coital fate. Great Literature is a hydrophobic in a swimming pool. Great Literature is an ant colony in a sock. Great Literature is a pencil made from biscuit crumbs. Great Literature is the unfunny racist skits on rap albums. Great Literature is a bookcase with 10cm between each shelf. Great Literature is a toilet clogged with geraniums. Great Literature is an unwashed sieve. Great Literature is an erudite conversation with a yeoman that ends with an inappropriate sexual advance. Great Literature is a student finishing a PhD on Kafka's women. Great Literature is a pushy Pynchon fanboy forcing *The Crying of Lot 49* on you. Great Literature is a cheese board. Great Literature is a man over 35 at a nightclub. Great Literature is an invisible pineapple on one's pillow. Great Literature is a drunk talking about politics. Great Literature is an undergraduate essay on *Wuthering Heights*. Great Literature is a Neutral Milk Hotel lyric embroidered on a cushion. Great Literature is a salamander in your blazer pocket. Great Literature is a politician who starts a sentence with 'Let me be clear,' and fails to turn himself transparent. Great Literature is a £2000 TV showing only *Ironside*. Great Literature is the kind of buffoon who italicises 'Ironside.' Great Literature is a podcast about pods. Great Literature is laughter at the expense of a broken man. Great Literature is an insincere remark made at a crime scene. Great Literature is a bowl of toenail clippings. Great Literature is a man from working class origins who is awkward around working class people. Great Literature is a hair-drier that blows maggots. Great Literature is a man who likes sharing his extensive knowledge on the Inca civilisation. Great Literature is a mother who uses the word 'cocksucker' in front of her kids. Great Literature is a religious edict that bans the use of root vegetables during sex. Great Literature is—"

"I'm leaving," Andrew said. As the door closed, I said, "Always works."

13

THE BEATING HEART of banality, routine, arrived in their tormentous lives. Holly, incapable of imagination except in matters of making pain, contrived eleven new torments and worked them into a timetable. One Wednesday, after Marcus had received nine whips on the knees for failing to balance a series of vases on hardbacks along his arms, he took Funkadelic, sleeping in her cot (a book-den with cardigans for bedding), for a walk around the children's fiction shelves, stepping over moaning whippees, seeking to avoid stumbling on Isobel and Raine in the act of coitus, which was taking place in the nook between the business and political non-fiction shelves. A long black coat had been tied between the two shelves, creating a private area where people could retreat to have half-an-hour's "isolation." All the couples used the zone for humping and the single people were too repulsed to sit in the secretions of lovers to use the area as a springboard for philosophical contemplation.

Mingling had taken place. Marcus met Gaelic scholar Phillip Diogenet and nodded along to his casual tutorial on Norse phonemes; museum curator Dringle Fortified and nodded along to his wisdom on the remnants of Pictish settlements; Orcadian battle re-enacter Cupola Bricksump and nodded along to his oration on the swansong Battle of Summerdale; newspaper editor Vivian Hershie and nodded along to her reflections on the unchanging vicissitudes of the island from the 1960s onwards; local fact-forager Timotie Doop and nodded along to his thirty-six observations about notable stuff that had happened in Kirkwall . . . begging for a swift murder with each nod of feigned interest.

Upon Isobel and Raine's return—her hair mussed and his shirt unbuttoned in a crude cliché of furtive rumpus—the couple had a squabble about the formal and stylistic inventiveness of Ali Smith.

"Derivativissimo," Raine dismissed.

"You can't pretend the smorgasbord of narrative styles in *Hotel World*, especially Clare's stream-of-consciousness expression of raw grief is anything other than a fat pie with marvellous and wow baked in," Isobel said.

"One word: *Ulysses*."

"Right. Yes. Because post-Joyce no one can use these techniques to differing ends."

"You can't bake them into a pie of sentimental bestseller drivel," Raine said. Isobel slapped him.

"Moron! *There but for the* is sentimental drivel? I can't believe I temporarily re-ignited my ardours for you through frustration at Marcus's temporary illiteracy," she said. Marcus was two inches away.

"All I am saying is *The Accidental* might succeed as a novel if the focus wasn't on a such a cast of bourgeois plonkers. Basic realist novel clad in postmodern cast-offs." Isobel slapped him again.

"WHAT?! Ali is a post-Derridean writer, you arrogant pimple. Parataxis took the taxi from Paris long ago. Her form is in perfect concord with her content. You have no clue as to the intricacy of her works."

"Intri*caca*cy," Raine punned, this time swerving the slap.

"Look. I can't tolerate this internment with mentalists. I need to check on the status of the parentus. Raine, all is forgiven with Ali. Take Funkadelic for a few hours while I sneak out to check on the wrinklies."

"You might die," Raine warned.

Isobel snatched Marcus and proceeded towards the fire exit.

14

"I NEED TO MAKE sure these greasy oinkers ain't shoving my frail elders into their gulag for the fabulous," Isobel said. She opened the emergency exit. Two sentries with firearms were each turning a corner in their scout round the building. Isobel removed her clipclop-prone clogs and Marcus his pat-a-pat-prone brogues. The two ran sockless into the street and took instant refuge in a bin shed. Negotiating the deserted streets, Isobel led them without incidence of death to her Mini Cooper.

"Is our marriage haemorrhaging?" Marcus asked on a road.

"Not haemorrhaging. More like sprawled bleeding on the pavement with a bullet in its belly," Isobel preferred.

"We have a daughter to raise."

"The best we can manage is to provide a convincing imitation of a set of functioning parents and hope the nipper turns out fine."

"I'm sure *Funkadelic* will turn out fine."

"We can abbreviate. Funka, Funky, Delia, etc."

"Delia. Let's call her that. On the birth certificate."

"Marcustard! *No* reading? You can't even skull-flex enuff to crack open one o' Vonnegut's wee pearls? Seriously, I know no human alive who would struggle to embrace that sliver of ecstasy, *Mother Night*. Marcus, you know there's nothing better in this world than worlds from words on pulp. You can visit Patagonia or the Great Wall of China or the Pyramids, but none of these nice views can compare to cracking open Beckett's *Molloy*, or Queneau's *Zazie*. I said this before, Marcumshot."

"Books represent reality."

"Books *are* reality. There's nothing else."

"Let me comprehend the illogic of that ill-logic."

"What's better? Looking at the Grand Canyon or reading a sublime prose description of the Grand Canyon from a master?"

"Both are equal."

"No."

"Is that it . . . *no?*"

"Yes."

". . ."

"Fine, eat this explain. All human existence is to be found in books. Most people are trapped in humdrum lives of economic uncertaintude, teetering along a precarious line of mediocrity, with their fruitless occupations, their uninteresting spouses, their insignificant children, and their repetitive vocalisations. Sure, people with a pot of millions can revel in the natural splendours of this universe, but, statistically, those with the means to do so are cold capitalist wanksticks, therefore lacking the aesthetic skills to appreciate this splendour. The solution to the predestination of life is to tilt one's head away from the inevitable crudheap of daily breathing on a tangible orb, and to read words in lines for many pages, to inhale their wonder, to lap them up like a moistureless manx a bowl of milk on a sunny day, and so on. Your notions of fathering without literature are bent. You will perish after months of silent sitting without the salve of Osman Lins. The reprieve of Raymond Federman. The sweet massage of Clive James. You think not reading will enhance your experience, will provide sufficient meaning in a life so far lived with a catastrophic degree of idiocy?"

"Your wifely counsel is comforting."

"Enough Marcasm. You know what I was like before books? I was Isobore. I was Isobarbaric. Then I read nightly for two annums, I plunged into the abyss. I emerged from that experience as the Isobelladonna beside you, presently thrusting this Mini into third gear to rescue her terrific parents. Books will make you, boyo, but if you refuse them, they will break you, yobbo. I have a copy of Lynne Tillman's *No Lease of Life* on the back seat. Open up that stunning comic performance and never look back."

"I—"

"Hold that thought."

Her parents' campsite was the epicentre of PiG tortures. The Prancers were, at present, being forced to leap through flaming hoops after completing sack races with toothbrushes in their mouths and X-Ray spex over their eyes. Helena Slattery, manager of the Phoenix Cinema, had tripped while making the final leap, and landed on the lower rim of the flaming hoop, setting her sack ablaze. On these occasions, a blind-folded OAP was handed a bucket of water, spun anticlockwise to the point of dizziness, and poked in the wrong direction toward the flaming victim. Responding to Helena's cries, the OAP panicked and tripped on a bump, the bucket and water flowing contrariwise to the intended area and soaking two daisies. The final recourse: two PiG beat the fire out with paddles. Two men therefore beat Helena and her fire in the sack with paddles until the screaming and the flaming ceased.

"We have to murder these bastards," Isobel remarked moderately.

On Writing

The Sack

I WOKE UP in a sack. The ends had been untied, allowing me to crawl into the light of a lifeless office. I stood up and flexed my limbs back into being. I could taste what I assumed was chloroform or a less famous volatile liquid. I munched on a Twix left on the desk. Then a man arrived.

"Ah! You've availed yourself of the Twix," the man said. I was too startled to recognise him at first: the baldest of the two bald councillors.

"Fuck was that?" I asked, spitting biscuit.

"Apologies for the sacknapping. You see, we can't publish this loony novel of yours. Can you imagine the public backlash? 'How can the council support this incoherent, self-indulgent nonsense? If I knew my hard-earned money was being funnelled into projects like this, I wouldn't hand over a single penny.' That sort of thing."

"You're a fucking baldhead," I said. It was the best I could muster with caramel round my lips and legs as stiff as choirmasters.

"Come now, I apologised. Let's skip to the civil part. Here's what we propose. You will remain in this room for two weeks. You will read the various books we leave you, learn from these, then we will send you home to write. You should have a clearer understanding of the sort of prose acceptable for the marketplace."

"You plan to what-a-bore me?"

"Pardon? Now here are the books." He removed from a box: *A Thousand Splendid Suns* by Khalid Hosseini, *One Day* by David Nicholls, *Me Before You* by Jojo Moyes, *The Alchemist* by Paulo Coelho, and sixteen even more execrable titles. I punched him in the cheek. Once down, I kicked him repeatedly in the side, until three security men bundled me back into the sack and removed him from the kicking radius. In the room was a microwave, and a second door that led towards a disabled toilet with a shower and fresh towels. Pillows and bedding had been left beside the sack. I had one window, looking five floors up onto overgrown marshland with a selection of decaying litter. Clearly, the hope was that I would be so bored staring at a slagheap for sixteen hours a day, I would cave in and read the books. Staring at a pile of overgrown weeds, muck, plastic bottles, wrappers, and other litter festering around a car tyre was far more pleasurable than coming within one step of those literary holocausts. I spent the day improvising conversations between my characters, randomly abusing the councillor for my own amusement, contriving scenes for the next two sections, eating microwave meals, jogging on the spot, taking four or five showers and, after three days, touching the books to see if I could create collages of superior value. It was a failure: there were literally no words in any of the books that could be improved by random reassemblage. Even the pronouns and articles resembled a tramp's face after an hour-long glassing from a Polish football gang. I broke the days down into these activities, and the fortnight passed. I tore the remaining books into pieces and stuffed them in the toilet, flushing as much as I could until the pipes were blocked. The security guards returned to bundle me back in the sack. I awoke in the toilets at Inverness Bus Station and made the trip back home, immediately resuming the next chapter of this novel.

Two hours later, I emailed the chapter to the councillor with the line: "Fit for the marketplace, Cheney?"

15

FURTHER TORTURES in the Prancer camp: strapping folk into rollerskates and forcing them to slalom blindfold round obelisks wrapped in barbed wire; suspending starved folk upside down on rope and dangling an unattainable egg sandwich over their heads; making folk recite the alphabet backwards and punching them in the face for each hesitation (one suggested on the phone by Holly); placing folk on a revolving plinth and firing milk into their mouths with a watercannon; binding folk to rocks and inviting feral cats to eat beef off their heads; strapping folk to enormous kites and launching them over the Broch of Borwick. Isobel located an uninvolved PiG and crept up behind him as he was carefully observing his colleagues and repeating their barked commands to appear relevant. She launched her hand over his mouth, poked a hairpin hard into his side, and said: "Move not, foul bacon."

Marcus helped drag the unresisting PiG to her Mini, where the pair bound his hands and legs with twine.

"Sadly for thou, I always keep a metre of twine in my boot," Isobel explained in case her captive was curious about the convenient presence of the twine. The PiG was Malcolm Headfortress, a schoolteacher.

"Listen, I can't be part of this PiG thing no more. We intended this as a kick in the cleft but . . . these roaring loons have taken it to a higher level of ouch. I want out. We need a plan. You need to stop these howling oxen of doom. I have an idea. Wait. Stop, Malcolm! No Malcolm. I need a plan. Wait! Stop, we have something . . ."

"Malcalm down! I have a plan. I intend to purchase a firearm and shoot them in the nipples."

"No, that's not sensible. Not sensible. I have a better solution to cease this syzygy of satan. I reckon we, that is, I, that is, you, that is, us, that is, meyouus, that is Iusmewe, that is wethemusmeI, that is—"

"Stop! Histrimoronic slug! I have solution of more effectivity, you stinging bumblebore. I will whisper it into this husband's auricles." She whispered into this husband's auricles.

"What?"

"That's right."

16

I SOBEL AND MARCUS slipped back into the library, where she wrote a note for Holly, leaving it on the librarian's counter:

> *Isobel Bartmel and Marcus Schott were seen sneaking around the Prancer camp yesterday at noon. If they are returned to you, I request the following torture: force them to construct a sailing vessel from books and launch them into the Atlantic to meet their watery deaths.* —Brian Moxhatts, PiG Leader

Morning snacktime: multipack cereals with no milk. Raine was feeding Funkadelic crushed Corn Flakes when Isobel sidled in with the neutral expression of a brown bear who knows the moose calf she intends to slaughter for supper, and sits in an unthreatening slump by the brambles as the moose frolic on the cool moss, waiting for the first set of stomach rumbles that will spark the swift and painful massacre. She had twenty-eight minutes with her child before Holly Polish, fresh from her canteen fry-up, plump and pumped up, arrived and read the fake note. She stomped over in her combat pantaloons and black tee and curled her index, summoning them to the beginning of their ends.

"You two numbskullistas will build a boat made from books. Orders from Moxhatts," she said.

"What?! A boat from books?! How?!" Isobel overacted.

"Stop hamming it up, meathead. Outside and build the boat. Two PiGs will point rifles at your anuses in case scarpering is up the sleeve."

A conversation began in the spitting rain about the books that would comprise the boat. Isobel thought of Ali Smith's "The Universal Story," where a vessel is constructed from various editions of *The Great Gatsby* and, pondering her hatred of Fitzgerald, rounded up his complete works to form the bottom boards. Isobel argued that Jackie Collins should form the forward and mast thwarts, i.e. the place to park one's arse while sailing, but Marcus said that Nicholson Baker was more apropos, as his works provided support and comfort over difficult trips. "You want to fart in Nicholson's face?" Isobel asked. "We won't necessarily pass wind on this trip," Marcus said. "We have two men pointing rifles at our anuses. The odds of not passing wind are remote," Isobel said. Marcus accepted Collins. For the centre thwart, a compromise was reached with the works of Mil Millington, as being something that one took comfort from and at the same time wanted to present to one's farting bottom.

The frame was made from the robust SF of J.G. Ballard, solid prose never prone to leaking. The mast, to which the halyard and sail were attached, was made from the works of Rabelais, Sterne, Diderot, and Dickens. And for various reasons: the bow—W.G. Sebald, the breasthook—Rikki Ducornet, the stem post—Kurt Vonnegut, the boom jaws—Zadie Smith, the stern thwart—David Foster Wallace, the sculling notch—Gore Vidal, the transom—Lucy Ellmann, the rubber gudgeon—John Kennedy Toole, the keel—Iain Banks, the stern—Alain Robbe-Grillet, the yard—Muriel Spark, the quarter knee—Philip Roth, the boom—Jonathan Swift, the rowlock—Anne Brontë, the hanging knee—John Cheever, the rising—Nicola Barker, the gunwale—Dubravka Ugrešić.

After two weeks, having exhausted Orkney's adhesive supplies, the vessel was afloat. Holly stood over the impressive book-boat, observing the strong bulk of hardback covers comprising the sides and the mashed-up, crinkled, papier-mâchéd pages that made up the other parts, and was satisfied that the thing would sink after five minutes and drown the pair. "You may board," she said. Isobel and Marcus took up their oars (Donald Barthelme), and began their trip. Holly, her sunken snout raised in sarcastic farewell, her scrofulous pigeon's twigs raised in a spiteful wave, stood on the edge of a rock (the boat had been launched from a small beach below the cliff face) and said: "Have a safe trip, now!" Isobel smirked. "Drabmouthed remark from that fist-faced cathedral of chunder. Now, let's talk about Mr. Curtz. Actually, his name is Simon Dennis Curtis. I refer to him as Mr. Curtz for obvious literary reasons.

This chap lives in a small apartment carved into the Old Man of Hoy
. . . you know, that coastal crumb with the face of Groucho Marx. He's
an ex-marine who moved up here for similar reasons to yourself, to find
peace and meditate, and read. I once visited his apartment and we had
a deep conversation about the loss of empathy in the modern novel,
and the impossibility of restoring sincerity to the text, in spite of the
attempts of Dave Eggers to incorporate postmodern knowingness and
a heart into his books. We had an hour of lovemaking that was perhaps

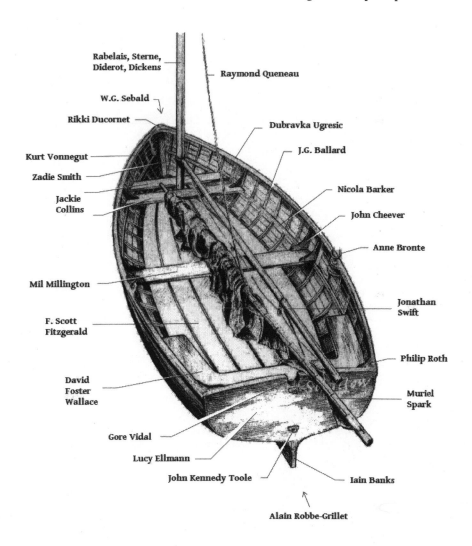

Rabelais, Sterne,
Diderot, Dickens

Raymond Queneau

W.G. Sebald

Rikki Ducornet

Dubravka Ugresic

J.G. Ballard

Kurt Vonnegut

Zadie Smith

Jackie
Collins

Nicola Barker

John Cheever

Anne Bronte

Mil Millington

Jonathan
Swift

F. Scott
Fitzgerald

Philip Roth

David
Foster
Wallace

Muriel
Spark

Gore Vidal

Lucy Ellmann

John Kennedy Toole

Iain Banks

Alain Robbe-Grillet

the finest I have ever undertaken in this short life," Isobel said. Marcus nodded. It was becoming normal to be undermined sexually by his wife with her every second utterance.

Isobel captained their ship, named the *Mare Librarium*, from the mainland, past the island of Burray, towards Hoy.

On Reading

Thinking Up Shit to Say at Book Groups

"SOME OF YOU," I said to the dwindling sum of some who were still present, "might attend book groups. I recommend avoiding these abominations, but if you find yourself desperate for any sort of conversation about books, here are some pointed pointers to ponder on. First, nobody wants to hear your endless nattering opinions on the characters' motives. No one is interested to know that you think Gerald acted like a spanner toward Hayley, or that Uncle Trevor was conceited to hide that secret from Auntie Penelope. You aren't there to talk soap opera. You are there to provide short, enticing summaries and reviews that will sell the book to other members. You aren't there to barely allude to the book and yammer about your own uninteresting life. To use a book group as a means of making friends, or to form gossiping circles, is to insult the efforts of all those authors by whom you pretend to be fascinated. You aren't there to be the smartest person in the room. If you have prepared material, or like to ramble on intellectually about the chosen texts in an far-too-erudite manner, you will poison yourself against the others. If you are the sort of unselfconscious oaf who fails to notice the looks of patient tolerance on everyone's face, the faux-interested nodding and eyes flitting across the room or staring into space, you aren't made for a book group. Do not choose one book per month. This is counterproductive. The ideal book group should consist of each member presenting a book on a chosen theme, that member offering the abovementioned summation, and after everyone's turn, participating in a general discussion on whatever strand of literature is that fortnight's topic. If the conversation descends into generalities, that is the time for the session to end. You are there to worship at the altar of literature, respect that sacred time. You should leave the room with recommendations galore, and perhaps with some of the books brought to the table (swap with regular members only). Extra tiplets: avoid quoting material on the back of the book. Avoid cribbing from Wikipedia. Avoid reading famous novels that everyone knows. Avoid fatuous bestsellers, mass-market material. Avoid bringing unusual out-of-print material from obscure writers. People will hate you for thinking yourself above them. Choose material accessible at any decent metropolitan central library. If you can't think up anything else to say, avoid aimless rambling. Do not use the phrases 'great read,' 'beach read,' 'good pageturner,' because that renders you contemptible. Do not turn up drunk. Do not attend if you are member of online forums for *Game of Thrones*, *Twilight*, or *Harry Potter*, or *Lord of the Rings*. Do not attempt to plug your self-published cop thriller. Do not flirt with anyone. Do not talk about politics. Do not dribble down your chin. End."

17

URING THE COASTING parts of their trip, Marcus read a few pages on the rising. Nicola Barker's monstrous comedies, with their hiccuping prose, their revue of loonies and oddballs, were a thing to behold. Twelve mashed-up pages of *Darkmans* was enough to convince Marcus.

"I must read more of this Cockernee schizoid," he said.

"Yes, reading Nicola is like having toffee larded into one's pores by a Grecian odalisque," Isobel added.

The Old Man of Hoy hove into view after four hours of oaring. Isobel texted Mr. Curtz: ITZ IZZIE!: LETZ GETZ BUZY. A door opened from ten feet up, and a buff bearded chap in a towel appeared and waved. The boat was moored after several failed flings of Raymond Queneau. Its occupants climbed over the rocks towards the Old Man. Mr. Curtz lowered a rope ladder. "It'z a zenzational Zunday!" Isobel said. Marcus made the assumption that replacing *s* with a *z* was a recurring source of amusement between the two, and hoped that the gag might cease after one more use. "It iz!" Mr. Curtz said. Marcus couldn't tell if the *s* had been swapped. "I have zuazagez for zupper!" he added. That was enough confirmation. Mr. Curtz kissed Isobel on the cheek and offered a manly shake to Marcuz.

Mr. Curtz's apartment had three floors carved into the rock. The first was a kitchen and dining area. "Hey there, Marcuz. Welcome to chez Curtz. You can see I have plumped for a sort of rococo aesthetic here," he said. Marcus wondered if that was supposed to be a pun on "rock." "I have a few porkers on the sizz here, I assume you two pirates are peckish?" Over a dinner of sausages, tomatoes, and sweet potato fries, the coup was discussed. "Speaking of porkers on the sizz, we need help overthrowing these PiGs. You have a plan?" Isobel asked. Mr. Curtz, shirtless, leaning back in his chair, permitting his pectorals a contemplative flex, his big beefcake face making shapes indicating thought, sat for a moment as Isobel forked the final zlice of zauzage into her mouth and after three moments he replied: "I have zomething."

"Zuccezz!" Izobel replied. She ran to embrace the beefman, leaping to his lap and hugging his bulk. Marcus worried that the two would start having sex on the floor in front of him and he would be unable to react.

The zomething Mr. Curtz had was a plan to transform the PiG into enlightened readers. He had in his possession a Mauser, into which he intended to load bullets made from pulped pages of the finest literature. The bullets, upon entering the heads of the PiG, would render them more intelligent, and less inclined to want to torture the whole island out of revenge for their being bland bastards. Having accepted the plan as one of zplendour, Isobel accepted Mr. Curtz's tour of the two floors. The next level was the living room: a chill-space where most of the reading and "philosofizzing" was conducted (Mr. Curtz's term for the violent froth of wisdom that enters his rocklike brain after reading Nietzsche *et al*). On his jagged walls: pictures of Gandhi, Mandela, and his mother Irene.

The top floor: a bedroom and en suite bathroom. A white-sheeted bed on the floor was all. Mr. Curtz had carved windows on each floor, and used rock-patterned curtains to perplex onlookers who suspected squattage. He regarded the bed and took Marcus into his confidence, i.e. wrapped a bicep round him.

"Marcus, Isobel and I have made love. I understand marriage is the union that binds you. But I want to make it clear. No secrets here. I made love with your wife when she wasn't your wife," he said.

"Yes, I know. I don't care," Marcus said. The bicep was warm and comforting. He felt tired and wanted to fall asleep on it.

"I sense umbrage. Listen. We are friends. Linked together by the same cosmic neurons that link peasants and kings. The lovemaking I had with Isobel was passionate. It was a frenzied storm of licking and panting. Our ardour built to such a pitch that upon the appeasement of penetration, we were one breath short of suffocation."

"Yes," Marcus said, closing his eyes. He wondered if he was being called a peasant in contrast to his king.

"It was that rare commingling of two bodies, in perfect sync, when upon the locking of cock and cunt, one is transported to heaven."

"Mmm."

"Anyway, let's make a start on taking back the island. You want a nap, little chap?" Marcus asked.

"Mmm," he said, falling asleep in Mr. Curtz's arms.

"You spiked his zausage with a sleeping wart," Isobel said.

"Yez." He placed Marcus on the floor and removed his trousers. Isobel was already naked on the bed. The licking and panting began.

18

FIVE HOURS LATER, Mr. Curtz was constructing book bullets from his copies of *Wuthering Heights*, *The Koran*, *Zen and the Art of Motorcycle Maintenance*, *Reading Lolita in Tehran*, and an unread *Infinite Jest*.

"You sure these will work? Might turn people into Koran-quoting zen Buddhists with a sentimental streak and fondness for tennis," Isobel said. Mr. Curtz made a "pah! nonsense!" motion with his manlier-than-most-men's hands, and continued ripping pages from these books, moulding them into papier-mâché bullets, and loading them into his Mauser. After nine hours of hard work followed by a break for bacon, fried eggs, tomatoes, and a sprig of lettuce, the Mausers were ready for use on the PiG.

"I like that fragrance," Mr. Curtz said, referring to the perfume Isobel was not wearing.

"Not wearing one. Must be my aura."

"The aura! The aura! The aura!" Mr. Curtz said.

"What do you mean, repeating 'the aura' like that?" Marcus asked.

"Yes, I have no idea what you mean when you repeat 'the aura!' like that. Is that a knowing wink to something?"

"No. Let's mosey."

"The *aura*?" Marcus muttered to Isobel *sotto voce* towards the ship.

"Incoherent. Must be the solitude."

On the return boat: an awkward exchange of looks between Isobel and Mr. Curtz, hinting at the shame behind their sexual encounter; a sneaking suspicion from Marcus that his sudden snooze was not down to tiredness; a silent contemplation of the loveliness of the landscape in contrast to the pending violence, and an unspoken concord that the world was a perpetual pull between beauty and ugliness; a posit from Mr. Curtz as to who would wield the Mauser and conduct most of the shootings; the embarrassed admission from Isobel and Marcus that they assumed Mr. Curtz would conduct the killings, having handled a Mauser before in the marines; a mock-enraged response from Mr. Curtz that it was assumed *he* would endanger his life; the slow obviousness that Mr. Curtz was kidding; the amused relief that he was willing to take on men with real machine guns while they hid in the library eating Rice Krispies.

On the mainland, Mr. Curtz began shooting the PiG with his Mauser. His aim was accurate: one book bullet into each member's forehead. As the bullet entered the brain, the pages soaked into the cerebrospinal fluid and absorbed into the frontal lobes, spreading their textual wisdom into the parts filled with loafing ignorance. He shot the two sentries outside the library, and headed inside to take out Holly.

On Writing

The Final Showdown (1)

N O CONTACT FOR a fortnight. I posted on my blog about how excited I was at the opportunity, and that the novel was progressing well. An attempt was being made to "forget" about me, in the hope that a media blackout would also make those who had followed the latest news on the novel also "forget," making publication unnecessary. I took to Twitter and Facebook and gummed up the respective walls with promo squibs, including excerpts from the novel, pictures of me walking around scenic scarps in a scarf, and corresponded with last year's winner and the handful of interested readers, and started flame-wars with bitter runners-up. This kept the publicity cogs turning. A week later, the second councillor turned up at my door in a porkpie hat, swigging not un-noxious liquid from a hipflask.

"S'hi s'hare," he said. He extended his left leg at a $37°$ angle, attempted a forward motion, and launched himself in a mad spurt at my bonsai tree, felling the pot and himself in a turmoil of mud and belching.

Eight hours later, I removed the mud from his mouth and poked him alive with a broom. He accepted the decaf and rotated his heels, slowly performing a graceless self-righting manoeuvre, spilling not a single drop in a redemptive show of liquid-saving dexterousness. On the pouffe, he introduced a dribble of hipflask.

"S'morning," he mouthed.

"Yes. So it's come to this, has it? My novel, simply for not being something Jodi Picoult might blurb for a fee, simply for not being something about which James Naughtie could speak in insultingly simplistic terms on *Meet the Author*, simply for not being something that might be included in a National Reading Week library display, simply for not being something that might be considered 'Important Literature' by an

Important Broadsheet Reviewer, simply for not being something that your mother could read without supreme bafflement, simply for not being something Stephen Fry would narrate as an audiobook, simply for not being something that could turn a man who never reads books to a rampant verbivore, simply for not being something that could be adapted into a vehicle for Ewan McGregor, simply for not being something that anyone, anywhere, in any country, of any background, of any race or creed, of any age or gender or education, would ever want to read, has turned you into a drunken wreck?"

"S'hole in one," he s'said.

"How many Tims? You need to sober up to the factish," I said.

"S'your talking like that bint in your s'book," he s'interrsupted.

"I know. It's addictive. Anyway, you need to wise up. No one, and I mean not a single mortal, and I include everyone who likes me, or pretends to like me, or knows me, or knew me, or pretends not to know me, cares if this book is published and released. There simply isn't a person out there to whom a new book means more than the author of that book. All those hours curled over the keys, summoning up clauses we think people will crowd around in ecstasy, thinking up phrases we think people will read and spontaneously burst into song, thinking up inventive structural techniques we think people will notice and rush into the street to tell people about: these are the delusions we use to keep ourselves chairbound. Of course, when the book is released, all those words and phrases we have surgically removed from our brains after painful procedures, are never appreciated, commented on, or even worse, criticised for being overwritten or self-indulgent. The most disappointing thing an author can do is to be published. Now, when you offer me the chance of a larger audience, you kick and scream and yowl when I dare to write something weird. Do you know what it's like for weirdo authors? We sit around hoping and praying our feeble strokes will merit a smile or an indifferent shrug. We live for the studied indifference and contempt of the reader. A hostile review makes us feel the whole enterprise was worthwhile. That's all we want, after the years of sweat, penury, delusion, self-hate, horrible loneliness, deleting and rewording, is for someone to say to us: 'Your book is a load of fucking shite. I much prefer Dan Brown.' That's enough for us. That is all we're entitled to . . . in fact, we aren't even entitled to that. We are lucky, the luckiest writers in the world, if an ordinary member of the public, who half-skims one book at Christmas, who would rather choke in his sleep than part with a penny to help the arts, who reaches for his triple-barrelled shotgun whenever he hears the word culture, who would sooner nibble on an electric eel than crack open an Oxford Classic, who walks past the high street bookstore with the shivering disregard a former alcoholic might have for a pub, when that Bob-Joe McPublic looks at our book, then up at us, and launches a full-throated gob of sputum into our appreciative eyes. That's what we dream about in our mouldy garrets. And now you, you slavering mongrel, with your knack for maintaining the monotonous status blah, with your 'love of reading,' if that reading happens to be the same council-approved books being hurled into our yawning maws time and again, you come to my festering hovel in a state of piss-misery, intending to beg me into writing a mediocre charity-shop backroom shitboiler, and expect me not to tell you to fuck the hell off my property, before I remove your left eyeball with tweezers, and grate your nutsack with a lemon zester?"

"S'zzz, s'zzz' s'zzz," the councillor s'snored.

19

S HE WAS WHIPPING Orcadian battle re-enacter Cupola Bricksump
with her belt for failing to pronounce the word "tergiversation"
when Mr. Curtz kicked open the door and unloaded a perfect shot
into her torturer's skull. Isobel and Marcus entered to help free the
hostages. General swooning occurred around the region of Mr. Curtz's
bicep, where male and female admirers perched to offer their thanks,
rub themselves up against the manliness, and absorb the aura. (The
aura! The aura! The aura!) His next task was to liberate the Prancer
camp. At the Broch of Gurness the humiliations were in full swing:
Denise Blatcher was tied to a Catherine wheel and having lemon curd
pumped at her face; Max Mouch was walking with two wine glasses
strapped to his feet across hot coals; Kevin Whitaker was into his fifteenth hour dancing La Vida Loca; Irene Pollox was swimming in a pad-
dling pool of porridge; Oliver Pringle was navigating a pogo stick along
the edge of a cliff; Thomas Brown was into his second week locked in a
public urinal listening to *The Best of Genesis*; Verne Oister was making
a porn film with his two ex-wives; Helen Driscoll was constructing an
IKEA table without instructions or the correct number of nuts; Kristen
Opal was on her ninth screening of the mid-nineties Robin Williams
vehicle *Patch Adams*; Liam Grahams was continuing to fake-smile to
postpone the electric shock he received when frowning; and Bob Gun-
ton was combing the landscape to collect his ninth dead bee to meet
the total of nine thousand to secure his release. Mr. Curtz put a stop to
this. He shot twenty PiG then went to the Hoxa Tearooms for lunch.
After a marvellous ham, cheddar and chutney sandwich, he stormed the
Trader camp.

The Traders had been put to work constructing the PiG temple,
the PiG HQ, and the PiG Social Club. The foundations had been set
for each when Mr. Curtz arrived to tackle the largest constituent of
PiG. Over 150 PiG were in the town hall at a meeting as Brian Mox-

hatts pointed at various manifesto pronouncements on a slideshow and aroused the responses "Yeeeaah!" and "Hmmm!" Mr. Curtz waited until the meeting was over and placed himself in the male toilets. During the social hours that followed, he waited until each PiG went for a piddle, shot them, posted their bodies out the windows, and repeated this process in the female loos. The mission complete, Mr. Curtz was treated to an expensive dinner at The Foveran Restaurant, funded by everyone rescued (which came to two pence per person), and was encouraged to make a speech at the town hall shindig after.

"Thanks, folks. It was no problem. I came here to meditate and read, so I would appreciate if everyone left me alone after this. Now, when the former PiG wake up, you will find them returned to normal, with the one notable difference: they shouldn't be tedious asshelmets. If any problems occur of a life-threatening nature, contact Isobel who will contact me who will contact someone else I know from the marines to sort it out instead of me. He might charge a fee. All right. Thanks. Have fun!"

The next morning, the released captives awoke with hangovers, and the piled-up ex-PiG moaned into consciousness. Isobel had driven with Raine to oversee the awaking of the people. The first to stand was George Cross, who around 5am stood and said: "Ooft. It's like *The Raft of the Medusa* out here."

"That's better," Isobel said, and went home to sleep.

20

D OMESTIC EXISTENCE inched along. Isobel and Raine sold their cottages and bought a larger house, moving in Marcus and Funkadelic. The set-up pleased Marcus, who feared having to cope with Isobellicose outbursts, and Raine, feeling the Isobellpull, went along with her plan to have him reintroduce literature to her husband in the hope of further intercourse. In the first month there were notable changes. The Swaddled Firkin, where once the colourless masses were hunched over swizzles lamenting their non-importance, was feverish with industry: novels, essays, stories, and poems were being written on notepads and laptops by the ex-PiG. Swizzles became tipples: whiskies, pints, ciders, shots to assist the creative process. Raine visited one evening and was stopped at the door by Dan O'Brien who was working on his first book *At Drown-Two-Cats.* "It's the sort of novel you might give to your daughter, if she's a dirty, boozy girl," he said with a wink. Raine read the opening page and pretended not to be impressed. Then he stepped into his own personal hell: a room aswarm with writers more talented than himself. Writers whose bibliography was not:

Novels:

Broken Cello (1992), Polyglum Books, Edinburgh.

Non-Fiction:

The Reading List: A Critical Dismantling (1996), Panclave, London.
100 Novels That Should Be Fisted to Death (2000), Outré Editions, Minnesota.
Read What You Are Told: A Philippic on the Evil of Prescribed Reading (2004), Bob's World, Ohio.
Jane Austen Must Die!: The Alternative to Eng Lit 101 (2009), Michael O'Morrow, London.
Cannoning the Canon (2015), Lulu, Self-Published.

Periodical (ed.):

Up Yer Syllabus (2003–)

The failure of his one novel, panned in four periodicals in 1992, made a sophomore effort impossible. *Broken Cello* was an opus. It was the fruit of a decade's labour: four failed versions and nine rewrites. It was supposed to establish him as a promising talent, and Frank Kuppner, Janice Galloway, A.L. Kennedy, and Brian McCabe napalmed the novel in their mannered reviewer's tongues, thinking themselves clever for stopping a new voice impinging on their latent careers. Raine included a novel from each of these writers in his *100 Novels That Should Be Fisted to Death*. He called Kuppner's *A Concussed History of Scotland* "a series of fragments from a concussed man unsure what a proper sentence looks like," Galloway's *Foreign Parts* a "lit-fic reworking of *Thelma & Louise* without the guts or glamour," Kennedy's *So I Am Glad* as a "superabundance of unstomachable über-literariness," and McCabe's *The Other McCoy* as a "proletarian snore from a dreary Carverite." He placed himself on the fringes of the Scottish scene as its fiercest critic, and boxed himself into the role of embittered loon with no chance of ever being accepted unless somehow his rants became popular via the blogosphere (their arch tone ensuring this was in no danger of happening).

He took a chair, sank two stouts, and noticed the island halfwit Clay Groober nearing with a notepad under his arm and pencil behind his ear. Seeking solace in the words of a witless nincompoop, he called Clay to his table, not realising Clay had been conscripted into the PiG as a human shield.

"Hey Clay! How many sacks today?" he asked, referring to mail.

"No idea. I resigned from my post the other day. I'm focusing on rewriting *The Grapes of Wrath* in dithryrambic form set in post-nuclear The Hague. Must rush. Adieu."

Raine ordered nine shots.

THE BIRTH OF
THE WRITER

I

A MORNING. RAINE, unshaven, spooned wheat rectangles into his mouth as Isobel scrambled eggs and suckled her newborn in a sling.

"Marcus in hiding?" he asked.

"He's writing a novel," Isobel said. Raine slapped his forehead and dug his nails into his cheeks and made a sound approximating to: "Ooaaahhhii." This sound meant that the two hundred ex-PiG were involved in, or had completed, over the two months since their mass shooting, substantial literary works in every conceivable form, and that Marcus's bandwagoning was a sign that even in his own shared home he wasn't safe from the scourge of assberets completing works better than *Broken Cello*.

"This artistic flourishing is terrific. But we've lost some serious heft in labour. Doctors, teachers, firepeople, sailors: a vast waddage of new-made writers, leaving bereft the island's public services. I had to wait one hour at the post office to secure a stamp," Isobel said. She noted the irony, adding: "An extra five minutes than usual. Hee-hum. Raine-maker, things are topsyturvying. You can't have a tooth extracted in pre-mium time. Bettie Orange is the lone oral option left and she spends an hour bumping her gums before flexing the pliers. Daniel Gruber is the last surgeon and the waiting list for the knife is longer than Pinocchio's hard-on. Iain Fortune kept the tourists well-lubed with his nous on Pictish potteries and whatnot. Now there's a nervous temp. Samantha Escort made the tastiest pork cheeks this side of a porker's profile. She's writing a novel about a feminist kickboxer with a penchant for Siberian anal. These valuabelles and valuablokes are sitting in bedsits hacking out mistresspieces and masterpisses. You hear that Candi Bokelove has been shortlisted for the Most Innovative Voice of the Year Award? She worked in the nail bar and thought David Coulthard was the Prime Minister."

"*Siberian anal?*"

"And that Paul Mugwimp, cleaned the local pool and moped around with a metal detector collecting shards of beaker: he's been considered for representation at the Wylie Agency, that hive of connivance!"

"There's a 'Most Innovative Voice of the Year Award'!?"

"There's a renaissance afoot. No longer will this islet remain under the tousled thumb of Sir George of Mackay of Brown. No longer will some bourgeois bint write a memoir about detoxing on the island in her friend's well-appointed cottage before moving back to London to pursue her journalism career. A hub is a-bubblin'. But that means we won't be able to so much as cough without fear of snuffin'."

"I'm depressed."

"Raine, I have said this a trillion times. Write another novel. Two and a half moping decades, penning payback pish for pill-literate dropouts. *Broken Cello* was a misunderstood sheaf of magnif. I assert this until my ass hurts."

"Yes, thank you. I'm have a lie down."

"Sweet screams."

On Writing

The Final Showdown (2)

"Good morning! You fell asleep, sir! Can I interest you in a second lesson of unpleasant rectal tootalage? No? All right, then! You think that these rants of mine bespeak of a mind ravaged by self-pity, that most contemptible of emotions, that I should pull my proverbials up, stiffen the upper proverbial, man up proverbially, and whichnow? You are a wretched legume in a botched casserole. For the one who courts countrywide acceptance, the easiest tack to take when confronted with the sea of begging arms, the sea of drowning authors, is to attack the penniless hordes as pathetic moaners, as pluck-free woundlickers, as castrated cruisers on the boulevard of broken losers. Your novel ain't marketable to the Serious Middlebrow Reader? Loser! Your novel ain't marketable to the Man on the Clapham Omnibus? Loser! Your novel ain't marketable to the Trendy Graduate Crowd? Loser! Your novel ain't marketable to an Able Marquis? Loser! Once an author has been 'found,' i.e. chosen as a sellable prospect by an agent or publisher, irrespective of the calibre of their work, and their material is on the shelves of a Major Retailer, there is no support, respect, or sympathy from them towards the unmarketable, market-hating weirdo authors, especially from the authors who market their books to the Market-Hating Weirdo Crowd. And their advice? Play the Game. Craftily tailor your creativity to suit a market, and pretend that your style of writing merely ended up popular by accident. Yeah, thanks!"

"Oh . . . stop . . . my head," the councillor said.

"And what do you think will be the consequence of publishing my novel? Let's explore the possibilities. The novel is published and announced. Copies are fired off to the reviewers. Boxes shipped to retailers. The first few reviews arrive. The reviewers, noting the novel's willed oddness, realise that some oik is attempting to halt the flow of comfortable Radio 4-friendly historical novels and memoirs, and email one another about the best plan of attack. They decide the best course is a lukewarm 2 to 3 star review, which sinks most novels upon arrival. One or two sacks of censure arrive from irate taxpayers, which can be placed immediately in the incinerator. My name is removed from the list of planned author events in the country, and the novel sinks into obscurity forever, until several decades later, when some strange dork obsessed with long-out-of-print novels from Scotland decides to write a blog about it, which no one reads, and fails to start a crowdfunder to republish the novel, and the novel vanishes again into the abyss. That sound more plausible than readers burning down your face?"

"Banging head . . . any aspirin?"

"OK. Posit this. The novel is received with rapturous acclaim. Zadie Smith and Paul Auster are sent copies and both spasm with amazement at the virtuoso talent on show, and yaddayack. You chumps look like visionaries for your forward thinking. I will, of course, inform the media that the council opposed the publication throughout the whole process, and tormented me into diluting my genius, but that's the fate you deserve."

"I'm dying . . . coffee?"

"No. I'll tell you something. Never has there been a worse time to be a writer. Books are oozing from pipe after pipe—"

"Oooohhh . . ."

"—a constant flow of literary sewage—"

"Noooooo . . ."

"—a endless morass of lexical filth—"

"Stop. Stop."

"—a bubbling swamp of rotting wordage—"

"Stop! Stop!"

2

Marcus maintained his reader's block was blameable on the absence of one specific kind of novel: the sort where a kind-hearted dropout writes an hilarious novel about a kind-hearted dropout writing an hilarious novel to win back his ex-lover. He believed that the ultra-subtle subtext might trickle into her awareness, and spur Sandra Acer into returning with ardour into his married arms. He tricked himself into believing that the ultra-subtle subtext might trickle into her awareness, and spur Sandra Acer into returning with ardour into his married arms. He pretended that he had tricked himself into believing that the ultra-subtle subtext might trickle into her awareness, and spur Sandra Acer into returning with ardour into his married arms. He found putting feelings on paper a curious business. To Isobel:

"It's strange. I can't write a sentence that makes me care about the characters. If I write 'she cried,' or 'she wailed in despair,' I know that in another moment I can write 'she laughed' or 'she hurt her cheeks with mad titters.' The fact I control their fates makes it impossible to see them as anything other than alphabetical characters poked into being with two index fingers and a thumb on the space bar."

"Yes, I have always," Isobel started, interrupting her sentence to munch on buttered toast, "said that more writers should stop to acknowledge their characters' cardboardity, their personnel's plasticity, their folks' fakitude. There is no fatter deception in a novel to have characters speaking 'like real people.' You have to be a massive pickle to believe that 'bringing to life' characters with the attempted parroting of mundane language is a desirable alternative to wholesale abandoning of the logic of human conversation in favour of a carnival of words rubbing up against each other like mongooses on heat. People like seeing their own mundane speech patterns in print. This preference has led to the artistic elevation of humdrum utterances made in one of the numerous predictable routines of existence. The future novel will consist of wrist-slashing colloquies on the weather's fondness for not conforming to MET office predictions, and a series of buzz phrases fed into the public's mouths from politicians via the media. In that way, we will arrive at the purest form of 'realism,' perhaps forcing the reader into more outré works to flee from the suicidal depression that will seep into their crania over time."

"So I remove all notable markers of being a human being from the novel?"

"Yep."

3

THAT MORNING on the island, a vintner was unable to provide wine for writing a treatise on the mental problems caused by excessive corkage; a sweet shop owner was unable to dispense bonbons for writing a *roman à clef* about the Yorkshire ripper's hamster; a hotel receptionist was unable to provide telephone bookings for writing a two-volume hagiography on the Baader-Meinhof group; a farmer was unable to herd sheep for writing a humorous sociocultural examination of the Orkneys from 2002 to the present; a schoolteacher was unable to impart the alphabet to cherubs for writing a novelette in homage to the precocious narrators of certain books by Belgian kook Amélie Nothomb; a pub landlord was unable to spout ill-informed political opinions for writing a trenchant anti-censorship satire crafted sans the letters C, F, K, and U; an oboist was unable to provide that sweet oboe salve for writing a philippic on the declining standards in woodwind competence in orchestras; an academic was unable to teach an online course on Renaissance Mannerist art for writing a book teaching kids the problems of flatulence featuring the character Frederick the Fart; a nurse was unable to take blood pressure and syringe ears for writing an epic poem in the Spenserian mode on Joseph Kony's atrocities; a car salesman was unable to lie about a Vauxhall's performance for writing an illustrated history on the correct uses of seppuku; a hobo unable to hobo for writing about hobos; and so on.

As the reformed PiG kickstarted an artistic revolution, the ex-captive folk loosed themselves from the responsible too, and capitalism ended. People took things for free without other people howling abuse at them for taking things for free, or people arresting them for taking things for free. Isobel went out in her shoes to peruse. At a local kirk, she observed the parish priest in intense conversation with toothless hag Margaret Dunlop, who was discoursing through her gums on the operatic mimesis in the sparse spaces of Cormac McCarthy, and the ailing parish beadle in a passionate exchange of thoughts with heartless crone Anne Stewart on Bae Suah's translations of Sebald to the Korean. At the Tesco, human beings, no longer customers, munched on apples and caramels and shared their favourite passages from the humanist comedies of Stefan Themerson with emphasis on the swansong masterpiece *Hobson's Island.* At the petrol station, people sat in the forecourt with notepads composing automatic haiku about their surroundings. On the streets, psychogeographers recorded their impressions of the landscape in diaries to be transcribed into impressionistic outpourings. A banner had been hung across the town hall with a quote from Ali Smith: "Books mean all possibilities. They mean moving out of yourself, losing yourself, dying of thirst and living to your full. They mean everything."

On Reading

Bookshops

"Y OU ARE WONDERING what I think about bookshops," I said to the workshop who were not wondering what I thought about anything. "You might think I am anti-corporate, pro-small business on this issue. The truth is I prop up both the corporates and the smalls. I prop up the monstrous tax-evaders like Amazon and purchase from the nano-cupboard of books two streets down from me. I have no loyalty, except to my own literary voracity. Like most omnireaders, I want as many books as possible at any one time, so I can't afford to have a conscience about picking up cheap used copies from that popular marketplace, I can't afford to spend full price at a local indie store on everything I read. Of course, this makes no difference, since the amount of money I consume on books reaches far beyond the casual reader, so I am supporting pretty much every outlet, because I am buying everything from everywhere. Those people to be despised are the casual readers who want to purchase books as cheaply as possible, even when they only read two or three per year. These are readers who place no value on literature. These are the sort of self-serving assbadgers who are willing to shell out £5.50 for a slice of cheesecake, even larger sums for unnecessary items of apparel, or £18.99 for a home-delivered pizza, but who refuse to cough up more than £2.81 for a novel. Spit on these people, rub expired liver on their faces. The trouble with the conglomerate bookshop is that all fiction is placed side by side: Wilbur Smith next to Zadie Smith, Danny Wallace next to David Foster Wallace, as if these two are of equal value. The mediocre efforts of celebrities, comedians, or public figures who write to further their careers and fatten their bank accounts, share shelves with the artists who write novels because they have things to scream and howl and mewl and hector at people, because without the forum for doing so their bodies would literally combust. I propose separating the hacks and chancers from the real writers. The finest small bookshops usually have meticulously edited shelves, free from the sort of popular sewage that clogs charity shop shelves, with something essential on every shelf. That brings us to the question of how to browse." I allowed the non-listeners a break from me making noises into the dead autumn air. "And back. Yes, browsing the book-shop can be fraught with problem thorns. The browser tends to spend his time reviewing the shelves, seeking authors she has already read, looking for titles already completed, often picking them up and staring at them as if waiting for someone to acknowledge his accomplishment. And she tends to scan the blurbs, looking for tantalising hooks, and he scans the first few lines, seeking a revelation right there in the shop. The fact is, it is only when these books are nestled in our laps, at such an angle that we can read the words, can we make up our minds on them. And as readers dwindle and dwindle, lost to the aggressive world of the internet and television and gaming, publishers are forced to make their covers as appealing as possible. Sadly, this means the peddling of moderately popular literary fiction that breaks even or makes a slight profit for the publisher in samey, uniform covers. Marketing departments have to speak directly to the intended audience, second-guessing the sort of thing that will sell, rather than allowing the audience to as-sess the quality themselves. There is hope in the small presses. So buy indiscriminately, buy even when your bank account is riddled with ze-roes and minuses. You can never waste a penny, even the chance to try a book you despise is worth the money, you fuckers."

4

"IT SEEMS TO ME," said the man behind the counter in a cornershop whose name was Lionel Avast, "that there is no one story in particular that would keep you rapt enough to fatten a folio."

"Explain, Lionel?" Raine asked. Lionel had read a short fiction that was to be the template for Raine's sophomore novel.

"It seems to me, and I am a mere man in a corner shop, that with your incessant listing of plots, ideas, sketches, and speculative fumbling, you are condemning yourself to the unpopular art of digression."

"Explain, Lionel?"

"It seems to me, and pardon these repetitions, that these lists bespeak of a weariness around the writing act. You are blasé about executing an idea in usual or unusual forms. You are a drunken moth making an unsuccessful flutter towards the lamp, landing with worn wings in the cold minestrone."

"Explain, Lionel?"

"It seems to me, and I seem to seem loads, that no simple elegant novels will pirouette from your fingertips, and that blasé bursts of huff-and-puff weirdness are the future of you. A Toyota Aygo in perpetual stall is the car you drive."

"Explain, Lionel?"

"It seems to me, and I am coming apart at the seems, that self-mulling fictions are your trade in socks. You walk in ill-fitting shoes, your ambidextrous feet guide you towards dead-ends, and you masturbate there, in bliss."

"The world is crawling with nonreaders."

"How so, chap?" Lionel asked.

"Like those so-called slacktivists, clicking on petitions, liking a million causes, sending two pounds a month to a mutt shelter, the nonreaders love surfing the web and sharing truisms from Harper Lee and Maya Angelou, showcasing their literariness through a sentence unread in its original context placed into an e-card with a cute font and a decorative border, stripping whatever meaning and potency the original might have had in favour of a TV sentiment unsupported by the merest caulking of thought."

"Hmm. You are posing the posit that people prefer to present the illusion of bookishness rather than being bookish in the real?"

"Yes. These nonreaders arrange meetings with each other, choosing the latest bustsellers to skim in the bath, congregating in coffee shops to reel off their opinions on the characters' motives and personalities for two minutes, before attending to the more important business of pointless blather over a panini."

"Hmm. You are noshing on the notion that people prefer to puff platitudes about books than presenting polished posits?"

"Yes. These nonreaders spend hours selecting the most irritating animated gifs to post on their online reviews of piss-poor romance novels, picking the shortest kindle stories to lambaste in a series of looping images featuring sitcom characters pulling shocked faces with unamusing captions below, extending in an infinite scroll down the page, inducing epileptic fits in the viewer."

"Hmm. You are licking the likelihood that people prefer embedding e-images into e-views than penning professional posts?"

"Yes. These nonreaders browse bookshops, pick up a classic and entertain the frightening thought of spending £2.50 to read one, then speed through the list of reasons against embarking upon *Our Mutual Friend* at this time—work commitments, TV commitments, timewasting on the net commitments—placing the forlorn Dickens back on the shelf in favour of a popular pop-sci title from a broadsheet columnist."

"You are stroking the certainty that people favour fatuous factual fodder in place of compendious classics?"

"Yes. These nonreaders skimread thrillers—"

"What about the nonwriters? You reckon these chaps rabbit on to newsagents with no intention of purchasing a paper, a caramel wafer, or a set of postage stamps?"

"You are positing the prospect that—"

"Purchase something please."

"I need nothing."

"Then leave, please."

"OK."

"Thank you."

5

A WRITERS' COMMUNE, *Furor Scribendi*, formed at the Broch of Gurness. The commune wrote a manifesto stating (in Latin again) that all their works were public domain and not in competition with each other, keeping their manuscripts in a special tent like ancient runes, mounted on makeshift plinths with the authors' names and titles on plaques below. Isobel wheeled Funkadelic towards the Creators' Hive-mind: a second tent speckled with desks where the writers wrote masterpieces with blissful ease on their laptops, all hooked up to a generator in an outbuilding. She pushed the pram past Fatima Grange, former nursery attendant, who was working on a biography of forgotten wit and suspense novelist Oswell Blakeston. Isobel had to tap the broad-shouldered kid-wrangler's pate to command attention.

"Oh! Hello, Isobel. I was so immersed in the Blakester's spiral-bound trailblazer *Magic Aftermath* that I neglected to acknowledge that pate tap!"

"Is the nursery still open?"

"No, we're writing at the moment."

"I have something I want to deposit in that building. You see the problem if no one is in there to handle my bundle."

"Did you know The Blakester wrote prolifically on cinema, cooking and cats, in addition to penning a double dozen of thrillers?"

"Yes, sounds like a regular *pisseur de copie*." This remark went unheeded, as Fatima was back in the 1930s with The Blakester.

This scene posing no more interest—over a hundred people hunched over laptops immersed in their own private visions—Isobel shrugged and made her exit. "I hope the books are more interesting than you lot," she said into the air. As she was leaving, she noticed Aaron Scumegg creeping into the manuscript room in his blue loafers, removing a folio and placing that folio into a folder, and placing that folioed-folder into a rucksack, and taking that rucksack with him to the exit.

"Hi Aaron!" she said, making Aaron aware that she'd peeped his folio-foldering antics, and him aware of her awareness.

On Writing

The Final Showdown (3)

THE BOMBED OFFICIAL was near tears after the first hour of relentless whingeing. He accepted the cup of water and two aspirin like a cracked sinner taking a sup of Holy Water from a benevolent priest. I allowed him five minutes of reprieve before I resumed the attack.

"Take my first novel, *Fat Battlements*. There was a 'launch' at a revolting artisan café, a place I had assumed I might find creative kinship, but where I discovered a roomful of falafel-chomping nouveau-trendies and students, completely indifferent to the art being performed around them but rapt at what their friend Kassandra had to say about her pet tarantula and which manga character was a suckerpunch to the patriarchy. As I read my funniest scenes aloud to these ignorant buffoons, most of whom by the third reading outright refused me even the basic courtesy of even shutting up for five minutes, I realised that the artistic world was entirely comprised of self-interested egomaniacs who pretended to be fascinated by other people's works to have some of the same pretend-interest bounced back at them. No other artist really cares about their contemporaries' efforts. The writer Paul Inch was *texting* during the second reading. I saw him yawning and texting. Probably writing 'a bit shit' to his wife, or 'defrost the chicken.' I spent two years in a mental clench so this halfwit could sit on his phone and undermine my struggle by texting inanities to his whoever? No respect."

"Stop moaning at me," the councillor pleaded.

"And after the 'launch,' I was patronised by Paul Fiddle in the *West Region Student NuView*, who called the novel 'infantile diversion in an era crying out for serious literature,' which was accurate, but that's for me to say, not him. And Emma Brodick on *Book Soup* said 'this is too low for me to hold it beneath contempt,' which almost made sense. And Geoff Pollox in the *BadReads Revoo* wrote 'At last! A novel for the long-neglected market of self-flagellating authors who loathe other people reading their books!' And my friends. Here's the thing. Your friends don't read your books. Your friends praise your efforts, buy copies, and make enthusiastic sounds. Do they *read* the novel? Nope!"

"You whine and whine and whine," he correctly observed.

"You know what writing is? Writing is sitting on a chair staring into space. Writing is two hours surfing the internet and five minutes typing. Writing is skim-reading 'writing advice' on websites and muttering 'fuck off' under your breath. Writing is looking at your friends' success and muttering 'fuck off' under your breath. Writing is reading over what you've written and thinking you're a genius. Writing is reading over what you've written and shouting 'fuck you' at the screen. Writing is £3500 college courses after which you pursue a career in telemarketing. Writing is something you either fucking do or you fucking don't. Writing is listening to Tom Waits and wanting to be the literary equivalent. Writing is ending up as the literary equivalent of Bananarama. Writing is forty publishers saying you do not meet our needs at this time. Writing is meeting no one's needs at any time. Writing is completing 2000 words one morning and weeping about never being able to write again the next. Writing is losing a whole day's work to a decrepit Dell laptop. Writing is never having the time to write and never writing when you have the time. Writing is having one idea and coasting on that for months until another one comes along. Writing is never having any ideas. Writing is sitting at a bus stop and having four million ideas and not having a notebook to hand. Writing is laughing at the sort of people who keep notebooks on them at all times as if they are proper writers. Writing is reading. Writing is reading. Writing is reading. Writin' is fightin'. Writing is writing."

"How fucking inspirational. God, you're an insufferable fartbag. I want a ferry, where's the ferry?"

"I'll find you a ferry."

6

"**M**UM, I AM surviving."
(In fact, I am beginning to feel irrelevant, like the protagonist in a novel supplanted by the other characters and plot events).

"I am still here."

(In fact, I'm not sure for how long. It's like a huge eraser is rubbing me out as I speak these very words).

"I am still me."

(In fact, I'm starting to question who "me" is, or was, and if I can refer to this "me" in future tense any more).

"I am . . ."

(In fact, I am struggling to utter a sentence of interest and fill the space to an acceptable conversational length.

"I . . ."

(I was Marcus Terence Schott, for 158 pages).

7

O N STUMBLING ITEMLESS from the cornershop, Raine observed Aaron Scumegg with his underarm folio moving along the pavement, his peepholes performing the frantic flit of a man doing something unfair with a stolen folder. Before being shot in the head by the pulped works of Charlotte Brontë, Robert M. Pirsig, Allah, Azar Nafisi, and David Foster Wallace, Aaron was among the local litterati, two *t*'s intended: a roundtable of untalented men with pens who praised their own works in exalted language, and slated the efforts of those who had not penetrated their pseudo-intellectual circle. Raine, for a regrettable two months, had lowered himself to their company, merely to feel part of something "creative." Since retiring from the local paper, Aaron reinvented himself on website Booklickers, creating an account with a bust of Titanic Greek deity Coeus as a profile photo, setting himself up as the world's foremost expert on each book reviewed. In a series of interminable, bloated and unamusing reviews, loaded with surplus links to music videos, online sources, and news articles, Aaron pontificated in short paragraphs the repackaged opinions on famous and obscure works, rambling on until the reader's scrolling finger ached, in an attempt to have the last word on every book, bragging about the bulk of likes received. Collecting a legion of fawning followers, too ill-read to whiff the overpowering stench of neediness in his words, and trolling those unfortunates who exposed his egocentric charlatanism, Aaron imposed his unfortunate presence on the website, changing his username to something more pompous once in a while to make himself more droll to his "fans."

Raine swerved to avoid the wretch, who deposited the folio in a postbox. Neither strained their necks to check whether the other had strained his neck to check the others' face for traces of a revolted look.

On Reading

Book Budget Mentality

"THIS BRINGS ME to an issue linked to book browsing," I said to the workshop who [insert amusing hateful reaction]. "The omnireader, over time, tends to weigh all purchases in terms of how many books they might have bought instead. This can cause trouble, especially in relationships. If I might evince a personal blob. I had a woman, way across town, who was bad to me, Alice Rìos. I was accused of being 'stingy,' because I refused to take her out for meals. I was always mentally calculating how many books things might cost me. One meal at a nice restaurant might stretch up to £50, which as we know, could equal up to fifteen books bought cheaply. Consider other purchases. New clothes. Why purchase a new pair of trousers when you can ask your mother to repair the rips and tears? A new pair could equal twelve books. And other choices: inexpensive freezer meals in place of fresh produce, leaving bulbs unreplaced for as long as possible, wearing two or three layers of clothing instead of putting the heating on, not drinking alcohol or leaving the flat to socialise ever, and walking everywhere in place of public transport. I considered these subversive acts against a system set up to hoover your money at every opportunity, and the purchasing only of books to be a revolutionary act. Sadly, when your girlfriend is Alice Rìos, this sort of activity is not conducive to a peaceful life, nor does society look upon you as anything less than a hopeless dropout. It doesn't matter if you spend your time reading the complete works of Dickens, Cervantes, Adair, or Brooke-Rose, if you sit there on your bed all day, you are useless leech of no use to anyone. I also, at the time of this relationship, refused to work. I chose the only form of freedom open to me: to loose myself from the responsibility of having to contribute to a society I loathed. I hoovered up the state handouts, eked a meagre existence on them, and allowed myself to be free by reading Great Literature all day in a hovel, while slowly losing the love and respect of a once-in-a-lifetime woman. A devotion to reading has its drawbacks. But society tells us if we work hard we can free ourselves. Becoming rich is the only way to free ourselves from the daily burden of survival. But the sort of people who work hard to become rich are the sort of people not interested in reading. And most people, by the time they have amassed a nest egg, are old and have less time left to read, and their eyes start failing them. Society says reading is a pastime. So fuck the rules, fuck everyone who tries to stand in your way. If you are a reader, or a creative artist, fiddle the system any way you can to make your lives tolerable."

8

A WEEK LATER, Aaron Scumegg's novel, *Tender Bunions*, was published in hardback by Faber & Faber, and a week later, rocketed to the top of the bestseller charts, following fawning reviews from Nicholas Lezard and Mark Lawson. This publication was in contravention of the commune's anti-commercial utopian ideals, and uproar roared up. One camp seized their manuscripts at once, and mailed them to publishers with their names scrawled in urgent caps on each page. One camp burned their manuscripts and put their pens down in protest. One camp opened a publisher and printer on the island and began professionally binding their own works, and pumping them out to London broadsheets for review. The commune's Golden Two Weeks were over.

In an even shorter time, longer than the implausible composition time of their collected works, the Orkney Renaissance (OR) was made apparent across the UK. The Old Guard, led by Ian McEwen, attempted to slap down the movement with patrician scurf in *Granta* and *The Guardian*. "This pop-up phenomenon will peter into the past like Pete Best and the lesser Beatles," he wrote, referencing his latest novel *The Grassy Car Park*, set in the Summer of Love and commenting on the seismic shift in cultural values between postwar blah and the emerging blah of feminism in a blah of modern blahness. Martin Amis appeared on Channel 4 News, and said to the semi-smirking face of Kristian Guru-Murthy: "We're sitting unworried at our desks awaiting the inevitable tsunami of cultural transience to wipe this fad from our purviews." Novels from the OR stormed the top-ten lists. George Ballast, former roadsweeper and owner of two malnourished terriers, became Britain's fastest selling crime writer, outclassing Ian Rankin's latest, *Goats Head Soup*.

Diane Riddles, former beautician and wearer of ten emoji tattoos, was the fastest selling historical novelist; Thorfin Caulk, former farmhand and sheep whisperer, was the fastest selling non-fiction writer;

Magnus Salles, former postman and paperclip hoarder, was the fastest selling sci-fi writer, and so on across the spectrum of literature, the same pattern of colourless human filler rising to the canonical. Scumegg appeared on BBC2's *The Culture Show* as the unofficial spokesman for the OR, having published the first novel. A sentence said: "We are the unpeeling of a powerful literary onion, rising from the sandstone streets to make you cry and leave a strong taste in your eyes."

9

SEEING SCUMEGG'S smug noggin on the box convinced him that order had to be restored. The noxious swathe of overproductive writers, hacking out timeless works week after week, was beginning to pummel the world of proper toilers, slouching before their laptops, wiping and unwiping random nouns to improve their flat sentences, clicking away from their novels to stare thoughtlessly at social media sites for hours: the real writers.

"Problem," Isobel said in the corridor as Raine articulated to her the notion of unshooting the talent from the staircase, "is that by relegating the virtuosos to bozos, a vast corpus of literature is corpsed."

"Then I can sweep in with that unwritten second novel and rise as the last remaining talent on the island as the others lapse back into their usuals."

"Have you been tippling?" she asked. The bellicose self-hoovering of his words was a tell-tale sign. "You Bolshevaccuuming?"

"Perhaps a Schlitz or four. Can you believe that scummy schlock-meister, ripping off Gertrude Stein and shooting to the top of the Fibber & Fibber list? I suppose one fraud begets another. And that Diane Pox-Riddles, riding the scuffed corpse of Thomas Cromwell, trying to steal Hilary's mantle with another 900-page slab of laboured nano-poetic prose: titillating the English reader with the belief that Great Men once lived two miles from their homes," Raine said, moving to the couch towards the middle of his second sentence, arriving there at the end of his fourth. "And that Thorfin Cock: imitating the slick magazine style of Tom Bissell with the pomposhitties of Susan Sontag. That man used to call his sheep 'darling.' And Magnus Sell-Out with his Platonovitudinous pap. Anyone can write an earth-shaking novel if a reclusive hunk shoots them in the head with the pulped works of Brontë, Pirsig, Allah, Nafisi, and Wallace."

"We'd have to," Isobel said, having moved from the stairs to the couch around the Tom Bissell portion of Raine's Schlitzcourse, "bother Mr. Curtz again and have him unshoot the island with some talent-cancelling pulp."

"Rowling? Sitting at her blotter shitting out Potter."

"Yes, or—"

"Wilbur Smith? Hack tourism writer incapable of pith."

"Yes, or—"

"Herman Wouk? Feeding us war propaganda until we puke."

"Yes, or—"

"Stephen King? Unfit to lick the boots of the smallest underling."

"Yes, or—"

"In fact, if I might pause this infinitely expandable list of drivelling illiteracy to address the Stephen King problem. All right, so you read one of his earlier novels, 'when he was a terrific writer,' or you have seen one of the film adaptations, each of them a vast improvement on the actual yellowing paperback originals and, coupled with his popularity, and recent attempts to claw back some cred by appearing in *McSweeney's* and other 'literary' periodicals (who are only publishing him to boost their sales), you have filed him in your mind as a 'serious novelist,' a title he is desperate to claim, publishing overlong historical epics and whatnot. But it's time to plop a North Korean nuke on this notion. It's time to perform Kim Jong-un jujitsu on this farce. Stephen King is untalented. Stephen King is a famous author, not a successful writer. There is no correlation between the two. King's clotted unstylish commercial prose is a product that will pass into insignificance like the VCR or the bagless hoover. King is a ludicrous oaf. He resembles a waxwork version of himself. That's what happens with a scorching ego. Begins to melt the person down. In a decade, King will be a lump of waxen flesh no bigger than a thimble. Perhaps then he will learn the value of restraint."

"Yes. But *The Shining* is amazing."

"Where were we?"

"You were taking lame potshots at the obvious unit-shifters with the arch laziness of a pissed troll."

"It's me, you know, on that Khaled Hosseini forum. They keep banning me, but I return weekly with a fresh email address, new username, and fresh torrents of swill to pour on that heart-tugging nonentitty. I would travel the length and breadth of the country, changing ISPs, to inflict pain on his lachrymaladjusted readers."

"You still intend to publish *The Collected Khaled Hosseini Forum Trollings*?"

"Several small Canadian presses have shown interest. Look, writing for me is two things: an act of genuflection, and an act of revenge. You lower yourself before the fiction-writing Gods, murmuring incantations of thanks in the hope a mere corpuscle of that wondrous talent might land on your shoulder. The bookcase is my altar. Every morning I kneel before the Masters—from Abish to Fuentes, Gass to Roubaud, Queneau to Swift, Themerson to Zamyatin—and murmur extolments. Then I open the laptop and right the wrongs that have been perpetrated upon these Immortals: I unleash heck on the hacks in book after book and post after post of unstoppable rage, summoning up as much toxic sputum as possible for one beleaguered old man, and in some minor way, correct the daily injustice that the aforementioned names are not on the lips of every boy, woman, man, and girl child-person."

"Where's Marcuspidor?"

"Within spitting distance, usually."

"He never really found his character. I suspect he may be trapped in colourless limbo, especially with the whole island turning into fascinating geniuses."

"We may become the dullest people here."

"Right, let's fix this fudge."

On Writing

Writing On

I WROTE FOR five months undisturbed. This means I wrote for a couple of hours on Mondays, Tuesdays, and Wednesdays, and spent the rest of the time staring at the screen like a toddler at a slideshow of the world's most gruesome autopsies, or reading in bed, or talking walks along the cliff edges in attempt to squeeze out something that might fill half a page, or having long online chats with other writers that fire me up to write absolutely nothing. I received an official letter around three months:

Dear To Whom,

It has come to our attention that you are writing a novel with guaranteed publication by a council-funded publisher, with guaranteed broadsheet review coverage, and guaranteed library and major retailer distribution, that is completely at odds with what we consider respectable contemporary literary fiction. I represent the Society of Bland Authors, a covert union that formed in 1988 to protect the rights of predictable and tedious modern writers. Our members include Tony Parsons, Ben Elton, and Nick Hornby. If you decide to publish a novel of a more sensible stripe that will appeal to more readers, we can offer you a lifetime membership.

SBA Membership includes: immediate placement of future manuscripts on the desks of the country's leading editors; blurbs and backing by some of the country's leading names like Julie Burchill and Stephen Fry; reviews from the top reviewers in the leading supplements and

broadsheets; a booking on the BBC's *Meet the Author* programme; booking at high-exposure literary festivals such
as Hay-on-Wye or Glasgow's Aye Write; the opportunity
to read in libraries and teach prestigious writing courses;
the publication of every novel written in the same voice regardless of quality or derivativeness; the chance to mingle
with famous authors at our Soho loft space.

Membership to this exclusive club is a sure-fire way to
maintain a successful and lucrative literary career in the
UK. Please consider this matter carefully.

Best regards

Aaron Boldlatch
Co-Director
Society of Bland Authors

Having reached Part Three, and with a few months left of the dead-
line, the chances of me whipping up an SBA success were nil. I kept the
letter to pull out in the future for a titter, or regard with howling angst,
and finished my valueless, market-averse, weird, far-too-short, dither-
ing, list-obsessed, achingly unfunny slab of tripe (not my words, these
were made in one of the pre-publication reviews), and sent it to the publisher. The publisher shared the novel with the councillors, marketers,
and the poet. Various remarks were made (in addition to the above),
some of which included:

"I can imagine this being sold on the street in a snot-covered hand-
stitched edition by a hopping mad hobo, not in a proper binding from a
proper publisher of proper adult people who read proper pissing books."

"This Poundland Pound think he's innovative? Dialogue chapters,
list chapters, internal monologue, self-mangling narrative . . . here's a
chump still seeking the approval of his sixth-form English teacher."

"POSTMODERNISM DIED IN THE LATE EIGHTIES
HOW MANY EFFING TIMES?!?!"

"Grannies in Morningside will redecorate their living room walls with this novel's splat."

"Students will see through its collegiate pretensions. Graduates will have moved on to Serious Lit and Classics or Not Reading. Twentysomething readers will laugh this off as infantile. Thirtysomething readers are too busy with their careers. Middle-aged readers are reading books about Deeper Meaning: this offers nothing profound. Older readers will roll their eyes at this undergraduate priapism. The Nearly Dying will use this to wipe their arses. Literally no appeal to anyone."

"The best thing about this novel's publication is it will keep the author's parents 'proud' of him. No, that's the only thing."

"Poisonous references to successful authors because the author isn't one of them . . . the sharp reek of bedsit envy."

"One kooky, zany, whackball noncharacter after another. Where the fuck is the human drama the human comedy the human humanity anything remotely human? ARGHARGHARGHARGH WHERES THE FUCKING BOOKER PRIZE WINNER?!?!?"

IO

FIRING UP HER mental rolodexedrine, Isobel isomerrily summoned up a man to mince the minds of the scribbling masses: Thorfin Furnace, an ex-pal of George Mackay Brown who slumbered in a shack on the lesser-known Orknook of Xness, an outcrop upon which Thorf perched in ligneous retreat, spending his twilight hours in contemplation of how repugnant the human race has become and has been from the beginning. He beat his chest as the waves crashed against his wooden snug, howling and screaming in cathartic spasms, his pained noises sometimes audible to the residents of the neighbouring cottages of Hollandstoun. Isobel's suggestion was to ". . . find this Thorfinned snark and arm him with several hundred semi-automatic uzis and whatnot and put a stop to this pump of pulp. I've been musing for the last three seconds, and I find these writers a pox on our progress. Masterpiss after masterpoop on the shelves . . . in the cashcow pile one week, in the remainder bin the next. A readership fattened on literary excellence, becoming blasé at the infinite innovation on offer. Raine, we need a sewage pipe of beststinkers to help us net the Golden Eggs among the Brown Turds. For every towering work of brilliance like Miklós Szentkuthy's *Prae*, there is an equivalent: a tedious mediocrity like Paul Ewen's *How to Be a Public Author*, or the novels of Dan Rhodes, for example. So: in a day or two, the first Orkney Lit Fest will be taking place, where London and New York's crème de McCrum will be in attendance. This is a fine opportunity for a cull."

"Now you're making noises that please my lugs," Raine said.

Harbourbound: a boatload of students on their summer breaks loaded with backpacks and laptops, making literary pilgrimages to the former sites of the OR (mere legend: pop-up towerblocks now sat on the sites, housing the authors who churned out masterworks for publishing imprints), having week-long sit-ins on the lawns across from the buildings in the sun, bogarting joints and writing their debut novels about fast-talking no-BS heroines in marketing who achieve success on their own terms (the females), and unhinged slacker males whose battles for self-actualisation are won in the arms of a cute pixie chick into Swans and Scott Walker (the males), before retreating to their comfortable parent-rented six-bed cottage to embark on the tedious sexual intrigues and failed fumblings of late-teenage life. The group, keen to mask the crisp diction that might mark them as home county Toryspawn, affected the blokespeak of a mid-nineties London indie band, fighting hard to widen their mouths to divert the poshisms of their horse-faced origins, and failing.

"We're up to check out what's 'appening in the scene 'ere," one girl whose name was clearly Forsythia said.

"I am afraid the publishers have filled the fields opposite their premises with landmines. Have a nice time," Isobel said.

"Is that true?" Raine asked.

"No idea. It's possible. So that response was both a snub and a friendly warning."

II

SPEEDBOATING ALONG the Kirkwall-Rapness route, blindsiding a few seals and zigzagging past a containment of toxic waste, the two arrived at Thorfin's shack.

"Isoooooobeeeeel!" came from within. A rake in a pinstripe suit emerged and helped Isobel climb up the rocks. She signalled for Raine to remain on the boat, neglecting to inform him that Thorfin loathed him like an ant loathes a rambler's boot.

"Goddaddy!" she squealed. (Thorfin being her Godfather). "You're well-suited."

"You expect me to lounge around in rags with a Crusoe beard like that Conrag Kurtz? Pphha! You know I would never lapse on respectable levels of self-grooming."

"Of course, GD."

"I see Raine the oozing sore is sitting on that speed. You still courting that omadhaun?"

"On weekends we spin The Who's *A Quick One* and tipple nine Rekorderligs. That can lead to unwelcome settee encounters powered by the potency of Keith Moon's pounding."

"I've been there. I despise commonplace utterances, and all utterances made by all humans, but it is lovely to see you again. I apologise for not having contacted you in nine years, but I despise the thought that some wretched millionaire might in some slight way benefit from me using any technology."

"My appearance at your door would have been toxic. Liking people and things locks you into begrudging cooperation in a world you despise. I'm only contacting you now because I need you to massacre three quarters of Orkney."

"Good heavens! This is the sort of visit I dream about. Do you remember 1998, when I massacred forty-nine dog walkers near my cottage? I liked to take an evening walk along the coast, completely alone, without interruptions. Then these wretched canine fellators arrived in their wax jackets and ironic bunnets, and let their vile slavering beasts roam free in my path, forcing me to interrupt the cohesive thought-stream I had developed to fake-smile at their odious owners, to pretend to find their filthy mutts charming. There is nothing more pathetic than another person imposing their pet upon you in public, and the interspecial blackmail implicit in these forced pleasantries. So as you know, I bought an Ural-smuggled uzi from George, and removed them indiscreetly from my purview."

"At that time George Mackay Brown had the world's largest collection of Ukrainian uzis, mortars, Ginsu knives, and pre-Zhou stabbing implements."

"Indeed. How can I help?"

"I accidentally turned most of the island into authors of staggering ability: rather strangely, considering the materials blown into their encephala. I assume *Infinite Jest* subsumed the lesser mâché."

"So the former numbskulls like Leslie Ploth are running around with the skills of learned men?"

"Who?"

"Leslie Ploth: manager at the Tesco. I went in one afternoon to return a botched spaghetti bolognese meal and Leslie made me stand outside his office for over an hour. Some of the pertinent info had rubbed off the receipt so he had to make several hundred calls to head office to check the procedure. As I stood there, with irritated shoppers and staff nudging past, I made a pledge to fuck the fuck off the island forthwithout a care, and spend the last four decades or so living in blissful fuckedoffness. No regrets. I was never refunded for the bolognese, which I poured on to his balding pate while he faked an eager-to-help smile. The idea that torrential idiot is in possession of a dfwian talent is incentive enough to slaughter the whole overrated Dorknay, that treeless flatland of impossible winds, Pictish pickaxe handles and stone villages, and the empty second homes of London stockbrokers."

On Writing
Dittoed Me Thwack

THE CHANCES of a straightforward publication were slim in the face of such momentous hostility to every single breath I took. I sent the MS to Giles Pediment, editor at Acacia Tree Press, and waited for their next move. I packed up and moved to Edinburgh to be near the publisher and the councillors. Acacia Tree Press was based in the Grassmarket region of Edinburgh which made stalking their movements simpler. I could position myself on the square and peek up at their second floor office with binoculars to observe their movements. The shredder had been placed by the window, which I watched to see if a print-out of my novel was one of the items being rendered stringy by a sexy temp. This approach lasted two days.

I tried a new one. A friend had been looking to kickstart her career in publishing in the hope of securing a home for her poetry collection *All Waters the Water*, a hydrofabulous selection of hippy-drippy sonnets, as I wrote for the blurb, and Acacia Tree Press had an unpaid temp position opening up, the sexy one at the window presumably having exhausted her patience at working eight hours for free without a single mention of scheduling her novel for publication. I asked Hortense (not her real name) to be my mole: to ferret through the folders and sniff out the evidence that I was being sold down the river on a flaming wicker raft packed with fourteen cans of gasoline. She agreed (for a fee).

Hortense was hired. I met her after work in the local cat café. She arrived with the face of a coal miner after a night of stifling subterranean lump-shifting and shooed a calico off her stool.

"That was like starring in six porn films while serving two restaurants full of fussy eaters while scaling Ben Nevis with a suction pad and a spoon," was the simile she chose.

"Welcome to the literary world, honeybeanpie," I remarked ironically, picking the hairs out of my soup.

"So I walked in that morning. Giles, that's the editard—or Gil for short—said to me 'hey, tempy, read this shite' and slumped over his laptop for a four-hour nap. The co-editard, Rosie Plonk—or Rozzer for long—said to me 'hey tempytits, edit this crime hack quack pap' and went for a two-hour brunch and three-hour lunch. Then the design-arse, Boz Larrtarr—or Boz for same—said to me 'temp, can't sketch this cover, knock up a design' and headed to the pub. Then the book-keeparse, Oliver Daomm—or Oliverrrrrrrrrrrr for elonged—said to me, 'you can add up, right? here's this year's books' and went to play *World of Warcraft* on his digibop. Then the marketards, Agnus Squint and Martha Hockies—or Cockface and Cockierface for nasties—said 'hey, come up with a plan for selling these forty,' and retired to an airing cupboard to hump. I was still reading the 'shite' Gil had slung me when he woke up. 'Read it yet?' he asked. 'Almost,' I said. 'WELL WHAT THE FUCK?!' he screamed. 'YOU WANT A CAREER IN PUBLISHING OR NOT?!' And the others entered and said 'WHAT THE FUCK?!' and 'WHAT THE FUCK?!' and 'WHAT THE FUCK?!' and 'WHAT THE FUCK?!' and 'WHAT THE FUCK?!' and 'WHAT THE FUCK?!' (that one from the janitor, Al Sop, who had asked me to mop the whole office with a broom), and that was the nicest part of the day," she said, stroking a ragdoll with a gentleness at variance with her demeanour. "After lunch—I didn't have one—the abuse of you via the abuse of me began. I was instructed to bend over the photocopier while each person in the office improvised an insult and thwacked me across the arse with a cricket bat. Gil called you a 'wart bursting open to reveal a flowering of maggots' and thwacked me hard. Rosie called you a 'tenement chancer with an intellectual canker' and thwacked me hard. Oliver called you a 'loveless tramp using our futures as a pissing station' and thwacked me ditto. Agnus called you 'the human manifestation of CJD' and dittoed me thwack. Martha called you 'the antidote to a strong pulsating erection' and dittoed dittoed me. Al called you a

'I have no idea who that is' and pinched my arse. The staff then made a papier-mâché you and set you on fire in a wicker candle-holder, chanting 'burn heathen! burn heathen! burn heathen!' and urinated on you to extinguish you. During this, I completed the accounts, knocked up a book cover, and edited a novel, and then was slapped for being lazy, shiftless, feckless, Generation Slouch, and pathetically underqualified."

"Ah."

"Before being tortured and worked ragged, I looked at Gil's emails. Here is one to the writer Callum Ledgie," she said.

"My nemefuckingsis," I fuckingsaid.

"Pardon?"

"He's a rival writer. He published his first novel, *The Green Grass of Hope* with Penguin a year before I published *Fat Battlements* with Three Quid Stereo. I went to university with him. I argued for obscurity, obliquity, and oddness in literature, he preferred honesty, emotionality, and accessibility. I argued that art should not patronise the reader by lowering the intellectual quotient, he argued that art should make itself universal and transparent or it was for an elite. He slept with Karen Blix when I wanted to sleep with Karen Blix. His remarks were laughed at more than my remarks were laughed at. You can see the pattern here. He also had a smug wink and a smug mouth among other smug features."

The email:

Dear Cal

Thanks for the MS!!! SO RELIEVED TO RE-CEIVE THIS. You won't believe the chaos this little punksquirt has caused with his wanky, campy, ranky, stinky novel about nothing save the contents of his navel. So we can FINALLY proceed with the plan to replace his snide shaving with this stunner. Your writing here, mate, is INCREDIBLE. Especially for something written in three months. One of your lovely lucid sentences eclipses a whole novel's worth of this halfwit's twiddling. TRUTH and BEAUTY and RESONANCE are the verities of GREAT LITERATURE, and you, my friend, have these in abundance. So here's the plan. We publish the novel under his name, but funnel the funds into your bank account. In a few years or so, the truth will probably have leaked out, and your name can appear on the reprint. Meanwhile, YOU WILL HAVE RAKED IN THE CASH. I know, I know, he will be hailed as "great new voice" and yadda yadda, but great new voices are leaking from every bahookie, so LAP UP THE MONEY. He will be exposed as a fraud and never publish ever again. HAPPY DAYS!

Best

Gil

"What's my next move?" I asked. A cat had perched itself across my soup bowl.

"We head to the printers. Replace the replaced novel with the original."

"De-replace?"

"Aye."

12

THORFIN'S CONVERSATION in the speed: the faux-poetic language that made *Broken Cello* a forgettable first novel; the recourse of ninth-rate writers to an output of score-settling bile on books better than those they will ever write; the sickness inherent in pretending to sleep with Muriel Spark while inside another woman; the inner angst of the failed novelist-turned-critic at always being on the outside of literary production; the rumours that certain people were ill-equipped in the trouser department and the impediment this caused to successful penetration; the fact that Raine was considered an intellectual on the island proving that the collective brainpower of the place was miles below sub-par; the fact that Raine was a colossal fopdoodle. Raine's conversation in the speed: the arrogance of people who choose to isolate themselves in self-made huts mounted on rocks; the cowardly resignation of people who live off the land and spend their time in pointless meditation; the presumption of people who have strong opinions on literature but haven't read a novel or experienced an iota of culture in a decade; the rudeness of weirdos who wash their clothes in the sea and make comments on other people's relationships, when said weirdos have no claim to understanding another human being, having removed themselves from that sphere long ago to live like a rock-hermit. Isobel's conversation: that these hypothetical people were sound chaps underneath and would probably work together to rid a certain island of a plague of prodigies, and that was that.

13

THORFIN SPENT no time partaking in the conveniences of cottage living. He had renounced the realm of inhuman easiness for a life of human freedom: swimming for hours in the ocean, hunting for fish in the ocean, screaming into the ocean to release his pre-free demons, taking mental trips while staring at the ocean, etcetera. The lure of a microwavable beef casserole; a programme about the Pre-Raphaelites on BBC4; the content purr of a lapped kitten; the scent of newly fabric conditioned pants on the line; the snug idyll of reading Cortázar in bed; a pot of morning coffee and a full inbox: none of these held a nanosecond's temptation for this man who had nonoed all the neat trappings of vanilla capitalism. He was the first post-human: a transcended being willing to wipe out an (our) inferior species.

"I have vaporised them all in my mind. This act of massacre will be nothing more than a twitch of the finger," he said.

The Orkney Lit Fest (abbreviation *sic*) was a facsimile of the Edinburgh International Book Festival (no abbreviation *sic*), Orkney having replaced the capital as the most happening place for literature, and the B&Bs swelled up with the usual revue of bankable faces, semi-popular names, council-backed newcomer "talent," and token European novelists. Situated in a Kirkwall field (on Dan Polyp's farm), the usual procession of pop-up marquees manned by recent Eng Lit graduates and unemployed actors sprawled across the land. The largest venue, formerly the Spiegeltent, now the Schaftent ("schaf" German for "sheep"—an amusing allusion to the change from metropolis to remote rural), contained the bar and seating area and housed the free events, ranging from poets reading their work on misunderstandings around contemporary gender politics, or politely disrespectful attacks on the present political regime, to new writers reading excerpts from their forthcoming inversions of the crime/historical/sci-fi novel with a view to being seen by the potential agents in the audience.

"You could start in there," Isobel said (having driven to the site that morning after a slice of square sausage, an orange squash, and some fried mushrooms—Thorfin ate some dried herring he had taken in his suit pocket), pointing to the Ovejatent where Derek Ghorf was in conversation with Mariella Frostrup about his series on the first transgendered African detective in Botswana, tantalising the middle-aged spinsters market. Thorfin had secreted his uzi in a special pouch Isobel had knitted into his right trouser leg and lined up for a ticket into the tent. As he was queuing up, he noticed Alexander McCall Smith teetering towards his front row seat, clearly plastered on naked apple cider. Mariella opened the conversation with an invitation for Derek to boast about the fan mail he received from Botswana.

"One little girl, barely literate, scribbled 'I loof oo' on a napkin and stole her mother's skimpy salary to pay the postage," Derek said.

"I hope you sent her a signed copy of the new book!" Mariella said. Derek made no response, so she moved on. "In the new novel—"

"FILTHY WELSH THIEF!" a voice howled. This voice was Alexander McCall Smith who sprung from his seat and shot Derek Ghorf with the pistol he had sewn into a fifth pocket in his blazer. Mariella hurled a clipboard at the Scottish author's head, the sharp corner connecting with the prefontal cortex, felling him on a row of abandoned seats, as the audience ran from the tent making various distressed sounds. Thorfin sat alone in his chair as the place was emptied, staring at the two corpses before him. He thought about gunning down Mariella Frostrup to have someone to gun down, but let the sex columnist and Anglo-Nordic bombshell survive, and moved on. "He isn't Welsh," muttered a tired OAP who was unimpressed by this piece of cheap theatre, and would be seeking a refund.

Raine was sat in the Schaftent enduring a neo-noir tale from a squat graduate with a bowler hat and cane, reassured at the sound of gunfire. The frantic Ghorf audience, taking cover in the Schaftent, were ssshhhed by the audience, who assumed seriously their responsibility to nurture new talent by sitting through readings of their drivel. The witnesses to horror politely located spare seats, their horror increasing as the Cramond cutie affected a Glasgow accent and pretended to be a violent hoodlum named Fingers McStab. Thorfin tried the Moutontent next where Sam Duncans, the author of poetic and topical novels such as *Nectar Lips* and *Turbine*, was in conversation with *Scotsman* literary editor Stuart Kelly. Thorfin stood up the moment Sam and Stuart walked on stage, but before he could fire, Ian McEwen arose from the front row, leapt on stage, and knifed Duncans in the heart, shouting something about his mortgage, and ran for the exit. Stuart Kelly, however, hurled a chair and knocked McEwen on the occiput. He then removed the knife from Duncans and stabbed McEwen several times in important organs. The crowd, once more, ran towards the Schaftent and were shushed. The reader believed people were rushing in to see him perform.

Thorfin walked to the communal toilets to release the contents of his bladder through his penis into an enamel bowl. He noticed Martin Amis towelling his ring finger so liquidated him for the kick. "That's for *Other People*," he said, referring to a terrible 1981 novel. Critic Nicholas Lezard heard the killing from the stall and nodded in assent when emerging. It became apparent that the previous literary establishment had plotted an ambush on the new one, with simultaneous bumpings-off taking place elsewhere: Ali Smith had rigged a bomb below Elsie Elfer's seat in the Caorachtent; Mil Millington hurled a spiked loafer at Bil Bommingtom in the Schapentent; Irvine Welsh fatally bearhugged Adam Oliphant in the Ovellatent; Deborah Levy launched an acid-tipped dagger at Barbara Strafe in the Fårtent; Amy Sackville hurled a Buckfast bottle at Sally Broker's head in the Pecoratent, and so on across all the flocculent marquees, most of the murderers avenged by the conversation chair, except Joyce MacMillan who leapt for cover behind the stage, allowing a blood-fisted Jackie Kay to flee as Regina Maine perished from a punched heart.

The reader in the Schaftent was now orating like a Shakespearean luvvie, livening his egregious tale with wild motions as the terrified listeners relived the shootings in their minds. Thorfin riddled him with bullets, causing a final mass stampede, bringing the first and last OBF to a conclusion. The echo of Next footwear stomping madly on oak panels lingered in the ears of those remaining for hours.

On Reading

Being a Literary "Snob"

"THERE ARE SOME fuckers," I said, trying to wake them up with profanities, "who hate the omnireader. You are looked upon as an elitist and a show-off and popularity will not purr on your lap like a tame kitten. You will encounter resentful, sneering non-readers who will look at you from their beery, leery eyes, as they might some form of sub-hominid anomaly, *bookimus maximus*. You will encounter redditters, youtubers, blogspotters, wordpressers, twitterers, and facebookers with wired-open eyes who will shout at from you from their crazy hectoring mouths about the liberal poison of literature. You will encounter the gamers with their twitching fingers who will look upon you as a character to lock crosshairs on and blow to smithereens. You will encounter the stoners and pill-poppers who will ignore you, and ask you if you have read Jack Keroauc's *On the Road*, and if you haven't, will lecture you for two hours on that novel and refuse to acknowledge any other books written by anyone ever. You will encounter the provincial retirees, who have spent a year reading *War & Peace*, who strike the attitude that completing that novel is a greater achievement than the thousands of books you have read, even though they lost themselves constantly throughout the book and hated the whole experience. You will encounter the self-obsessed students whose radical interpretations of *Agnes Grey* and *The Idiot* are the most important utterance anyone anywhere has ever made with their mouths, while ignoring the thousands of novels you have read. You will encounter the parents and siblings who take every literary reference you make back to the several books they enjoyed reading as a child, and then redirect the conversation to what TV shows they have been watching. You will encounter the teachers and lecturers, for whom any text not on their syllabus is a waste of time, and look upon you as a wayward student in need of their salvation.

You will encounter the travellers and backpackers who will take pity on you for wasting your life, then tell you about the Paulo Coelho they read while hostelling across Europe en route to their spiritual pilgrimage to New Delhi. You will encounter the hard-working moaners who will tell you they are too busy working for a living to sit and read all day, and when they come home from a hard day's toil, they don't want to sit and read pretentious rubbish. You will encounter the voracious readers who loathe competition, and who will challenge you to a literary duel, rather than engage you in friendly conversation about your latest reading. You will encounter the slack intellectuals who will immediately ask you if you have read *Finnegans Wake*, and when you say you have, will ask if you if you understood every line, and when you say of course not, will make some point that generally alludes to you being a halfwit. Fuck those fuckers."

14

IN THE CRABBED SATCHEL, over two VIIs, Thorfin and Isobel moped and celebrated and moped respectively, the former at his pitiful kill rate, the latter having rid the island of the too-talented upstarts and the needless slaughter of a fraction of some of her favourite novelists.

"I suppose I should feel remorse at having set in motion the chain of events that led to this disgusting afternoon," she said. "However, I think this outcome is a natural symptom of island life. A similar thing happened in Shetland in the early 1990s, when a spontaneous rave scene kicked off, and the whole island OD'd to the Happy Mondays' . . . *Yes Please*, ellipsis *sic*."

"It *was* a terrible album," Thorfin said.

"If I hadn't intervened, the PiG might have invaded Thurso and launched a full-scale war on the North Highlands. At least we have a catalogue of memorable masterpieces to devour as a legacy, rather than the random brains of crofters splattered over the feeding troughs of Angus cows," she observed.

"Is there anyone left to shoot?" Thorfin asked.

"Better case the slugs, Goddaddio. We need to repopulate our shops and industries, or the island will wither. Or even worse, will be put up for sale, like how the Isle of Man was sold to Richard Branson after their 2013 kabuki massacre."

"Who will replenish Britain's literature business?"

"There are a few new bids on the cock," a voice said from the bar. That voice was attached to a person who turned round to reveal himself to be Marcus Schott, former protagonist of this novel. Sporting a Stetson, casual wool waistcoat, blue jeans, and a pair of brown wrangler slips, Marcus approached the table, howdytipping the hat, and tabling a novel called *Hell's Angles* by Marcus T. Schott about a band of renegade mathematicians who raised heck on the prairie and set the foundations for later proofs of Fermat's last theorem.

"Marcusk-eel! So pleasant to see you here, and not not-seeing you not helping raise the Funkadelic your daughter!"

"I had to take some time for myself."

"And in that time, you shot yourself in the head with Mr. Curtz's pulp, turned yourself into a Scots-Western novelist, and now you're cultivating a public image as a local cowboy author?"

"As usual, your summation powers are supremo."

"Can I shoot this gobsheen?" Thorfin asked.

"No, I have one spawn with this man."

"Where is Funkadelic?" Marcus T. Schott asked.

"Parents."

"Of course. Now, let's plot a course into the new time. I have funds, I have cred. I can toss off these bestselling Scots-Westerns in a few months. I can devote my time to finally reading Peter Boxall's *1001 Books You Must Read Before You Die*."

"Sweet Lordfuck," Thorfin said, raising the uzi.

"No! No parricide, GD. Remember the time you stabbed Len Gormand in the clavicle because he sneaked into your parking space? His son posted a turd through your letter box every day, causing the postman to despise you, and he in turn began urinating through your letter box every day, causing your cat to despise you, and he in turn began to scratch you while you were sleeping. You had to blast them apart, except the cat, which you placed with a cat charity, then adopted by the kindly Mrs. Grommit."

"Yes. It was a shame she fell asleep and crushed it on the first night."

15

A LONG WRANGLE began as to which of the sponsors should cough up to remove the corpses from the OBF site. RBS produced an 100-page treatise arguing the legal *lacunae* of the situation absolved them from responsibility; The University of Highlands & Islands produced a 101-page treatise attempting to shift the *onus probandi* on to Walter Scott Global Investment Management who in turn attempted to blame the principal funders *per incurium*; Baillie Gifford preferred to keep the whole event concealed from public view in an act of *suppressio veri*; People's Postcode Lottery chose to blame the farmer, Dan Polyp, on whose land the event had been held, citing *cuius est solum eius est usque ad coelum et ad inferos*; Creative Scotland chose to attack the Scottish Government in a scurrilous online hate campaign, claiming the First Minister had acted *contra bonos mores*; and the British Academy stuck the legal knife into Woodland Trust Scotland, claiming they had acted *animus nocendi*. Meanwhile the seagulls feasted on the corpses, with Ian Rankin the first to be pecked clean: a complicit act between the birds that made the locals admire their sound judgement.

Marcus swooped on the opportunity to exploit the massacre, appearing on TV as the lone survivor (he had been in the bar at the time, his novel having been published too late to arrange an OBF slot), expressing his horror at the wasted talents while hinting that certain people had survived to keep the torch of Great Literature alive. In a candid interview with Mark Lawson, he revealed how he had cradled Graham Swift in his arms as the author wheezed his last and pledged that he would never let the legacies of these wonderful writers fade: he intended to continue their work and had begun with his first novel *Hell's Angles* that had been compared to Pythagoras and Cormac McCarthy.

Around this time, Raine had sank into steep melancholia. The combination of Thorfin who, upon seeing Funkadelic, chose to take the spare room and coo at the tyke, and at meals insult Raine's literary

impotence; and Marcus's unfair success and attention-seeking, inten-
sified an already two-decade-long need to salve the itch of life. One
afternoon Isobel observed that Raine hadn't been in the house for two
twelve-hour periods. He had stepped out after a bowl of Coco Pops the
previous morning.

On Writing

Vickers & Daughter

THE PRINTER was Gregor Vickers & Daughter. Gregor Vickers had risen to prominence for his handbound art books, and opened up a printing firm for some of the top local publishers with his daughter Spacey. Hortense was familiar with Spacey, an artist noted for her Artistically Significant monochrome photographs of random objects on street pavements that had been reviewed in *The Independent* as "daring" and "stark," and known for being, in Hortense's words, a conceited fuck-weasel. We contrived plans of assault, such as committing actual assault on the owners, seducing them with our bodies, begging on our knees, performing emotional numbers on a balalaika, or offering them free tickets to panto for a year. In the end, it made more sense to walk in and ask them if:

"My publisher is trying to suppress my novel," I said to Gregor Vickers, a lank man with a moustache working on a woodcut.

"How?"

"Because they hate anything that can't be marketed with an acacia tree."

"Oh."

"So I need you to print this manuscript and not the one they sent you."

"Why?"

"Because I wrote this one and they're putting my name on the cover."

"Right."

"Will you do it, then?"

"What?"

"Publish the proper novel?"

"Sure."

"WAIT!!!" Spacey boomed. She appeared from a room in a black frock and sneakers with an Arthurian tattoo on her left arm. "Dad, you can't let someone stroll in and change the whole text of a book."

"Hi, I'm the author," I said. Outstretched paw ignored.

"He says he's the author and that this publisher is attempting to replace his text with something else. I can't imagine why someone would walk in here and make that up. Such an occurrence is even beyond the realm of some unfunny depiction of the mentally ill in a novel that a lesser writer might write."

"Dad, we are contractually bound to put out whatever Acacia Tree Press are paying us to print."

"What can we do for you?" Hortense asked. She had been standing beside me the whole time but hadn't spoken until that point.

"You know my photographs have been acclaimed in *The Independent*?"

"Yes," I lied.

"I'm planning to publish a collection in a deluxe hardback book and want to promote its release by showcasing some elsewhere. Put five or six in your book and we might have a deal. Also, I'd like £3,000."

"Fine," I said, having £2,999.50 of the prize money remaining.*

"Hortense, do you have 50p?" I asked. She produced that sum. I handed the coin to Spacey. "The rest can be paid by bank transfer."

"Thank you. Hand me the USB with your manuscript. I can reformat the thing to add my photos. When the money appears, we'll print the original."

"Grateful."

I left and went to bar to spend the rest of my money on ethanol products.

*See Appendix.

16

ACHOCOMILK BURP sent Raine into the whatever wind of an October morning. The sound of Marcus hammering on his keyboard sentences that soared above whatever mediocre mashed potato sat on his long-closed laptop sent him lunging for his coat and the front door, in a state of literal and metaphorical and violent nausea. He skirted along the cliff edges, the unpeggable odour of putrescent corpses of former Booker Prize winners and unrealised upcoming talent in his nose, waiting for the right spot for an aerial passing into the nothing. He chose the one with the fewest protruding rocks, opening up the chance for survival, then put "50ft Queenie" by PJ Harvey on the ipod, leaping around in spasms to the music, working himself into a hexagonal froth and hurling himself off the cliff at the song's climax. No one except cliff suicide survivors with refined prose composition abilities can render the sensation of throwing oneself on the mercy of gravitational chance.

Raine fell. The hard slap of the water on his skull was a sufficient killer, and Raine perished instantly. The police visited Isobel the following week, informing her that his ipod had been found washed up on shuffle.

"What track was playing?" she asked.

"I believe it was 'All That She Wants' by Ace of Base."

"Thank you," she said, closing the door. "That's the unmaking of poor Raine. Maddening moping mercurial man among men." She sat and cried for an hour. Marcus swaggered in chomping on an apple.

"That's me clacked out another 10K of the new one, *A Fistful of Quasars*. I can see the reviews now. Prof. Brian Cox: 'This luminous epic matches the machismo of Eastwood with the astrological deductions of Sir Roger Penrose.' Steven Moore: 'A sensational performance that takes the theatrics of a Morricone score and ties them to Sir Patrick Moore's monocle.' I tell you, shooting myself in the head was the finest move I ever made. The literary world has a new force to reckon with and his name is Marcus T.—"

Isobel slapped Schott hard and stropped off.

17

ER ISOCEREBELLUM was abulge with verbal gunge. She biked to her parents at the Broch and hugged their bones. "Motherkins and Paparazzo, I need the new. Raine snuffed himself and Marcus is a bloated bore and Thorfin is obsessed with tickling Funk. I can't live in these condireshits. I am on Ferry Next. You have one option in two parts: remain here, or remain here in spirit and come with me to a metropolis."

"Darling we are wrinkled ogres with our clodhoppers in cement. We couldn't recalibrate our brains to the fast-paced car-packed scream of Big Town," Mother said.

"But we fathom the need to free. Honey, we support whatever trans-plantsubstantiation is needed," Father said.

She spent the day with them reading Josef Škvorecký, listening to Kristin Hersh, and slurping onion soup.

On Writing

Snublication

I EXPECTED the marketers would riddle me with pellets. I expected the councillors would incarcerate me in a minute cubicle. I expected the publisher would mail me a bill for five thousand or more pounds. I expected the police would insert their truncheons into unguarded orifices. I expected the reviewers to unearth the scandal and lacerate me with their well-phrased barbs. I expected the readers to hurl pebbles at me in the street and spit at me on the bus and stab me in the corridor and urinate on me in the casket. As usual, I expected too much from publication. I expected *something*. The publishers and marketers and councillors and other middlemen who had perched their fat butts on my novel from day one, had at last twigged that the easiest option was to allow the novel to make its own way in the world. I received my fifty author copies, and awaited information about a launch or a lunch or an inch of action to be taken. Nothing. I scooped up the country's top literary magazines, the country's middling literary pamphlets, and the country's least-clicked literary sites for a whiff of acknowledgement. The silence had me begging for the shortest flagellation from the most patronising and ill-read populist. After two months, on *Shazza's Top Reads* site, a personal blog, I found a short paragraph: "Someone handeded [*sic*] me this book to read. I skimmed thru [*sic*] and it looks annoying."

Thanks, Shazza.

Later, I spoke to Hortense, who had been temping for one of Scotland's premier reviewing pipes. She explained:

"The editors received the book with bafflement. No one understood what the novel was. No one was sure whether it was a novel at all. Rather than have reviewers savage the 'thing' and risk the council cutting the funding to fine reviewing organs like theirs, the editors collaborated in a 'circle shirk,' leaving the book to rot unassigned in their cabinets and cupboards, and this trickled down to the other reviewing venues—most of whom attempt to leech readers from the larger circulation magazines by commenting on the same hot topics—who had no means of increasing their readership in praising your book. And for the independent zines covering off-beat small press material, well, your book was too high-profile for them. That left the bottom-feeding bloggers and online reviewers, known as the 'scum-sucking bedsit no-hopers' to the editors, who for the most part like to air their thoughts on what is popular (to attract attention to themselves and to keep abreast of the zeitgeist being fed to them by corporations). That's how Shazza ended up as the one human on the planet to mention your book at all. You've been snublished."

"*Que?*"

"Snublished is what the presses call the process of not-promoting-on-purpose a novel."

"Good to know."

I received a formal letter six months later, informing me that the initial print run had sold poorly, and that the novel would not be published in paperback, and that the rights to the text had reverted to me. I chose to reissue the novel with this explanatory matter included from the publisher who has published this "thing" you are reading now. And that, my friends, brings this clatter around to the long-awaited shush.

18

R AINE HAD OVER a thousand suggestions for his funeral on walled post-its, in his notebooks, and the subfolder FUNERAL in his large DEATH file, including "in the event of my passing please": locate Nick Hornby and punch him in the limbs; suspend my corpse above 100 smouldering copies of *Atlas Shrugged* and lower me into the flames; order a pizza for the vicar before the ceremony, so the delivery man interrupts the reverence with a ham and pineapple; insist that the whole Joy Division album *Closer* be played at the end of the ceremony, and seal the doors shut; invite a local gutter poet to recite one of his nine-minute "Odes to Fucking" after my mother's tribute; arrange for a heckler in the back row to hurl well-timed insults about me at the most tender moments; have four arthritic old men as pallbearers so the coffin is shattered on the floor and my corpse bursts out; have the priest read out my "What I Really Think of You Cunts" file as I am lowered into the ground; force my mother to read one of my whole books to the end in the middle of the mass, and not let anyone out until she makes a semi-complimentary remark; hire a thug to beat the vicar into admitting that God is nonexistent and religions are corrupt property rackets; interrogate the guests as to what books they have actually read, those they have pretended to read, and those they have actually enjoyed and those they have pretended to enjoy, using torture if necessary to make them confess; have my stuffed corpse mounted at Kirkwall pier, so the first thing incoming ferries see is my miserable naked form, reminding the islanders that they are responsible for my death; make academic Paul Inchcolm confess that Nabokov's *Ada or Ardor: A Family Chronicle* is unreadable shite; hack me up, throw me in a binliner, and hurl me into the sea like Robert Durst's old neighbour; have my corpse inflated and suspended above the room, with an advert for Mabel's Dry Cleaning pinned along my torso; pass a collection round to raise funds for sharp implements with which to spear Lee Child; and another 989 examples of things to happen with his remains and the remaining.

Isobel opened the "What I Really Think of You Cunts" file and read the printed form of the bilious bomblast he had been making for annums with a fresh flash of pathos and scrolled to the entry on herself. "Isobel Bartmel. Muse and Medusa. Over a decade, I have tussled with this tousled tosser. We have exchanged flaming spears of discourse over the amateur knitting of David Mitchell, the lukewarm roulade of Jonathan Safran Foer, the dented bumper of Austryn Wainhouse, the snapped vertebrae of Paul Torday, the shattered plasma of Kathy Lette, and the bagless vacuum of Bill Bryson. We have spent evenings reading loud the hallowed prose of Paul West, Vedrana Rudan, Flann O'Brien. We have also made love atop a beached whale off the Broch of Burness. We have slapped each other in the face at the Pictish village and been banned forever. We have broken in to the bakery to eat pastries at sundown after a night on the lash. These and many other things have made my time with this irritating and incredible nitwonder something to remember. There's one final remark I want to make about Isobel, which is—." At which point the page was torn. Isobel knew that Raine had ripped the page out on purpose to irritate her, to leave her questioning her whole life what he really thought about her.

"I . . . . you too," she said.

19

S HE HAD HIM CREMATED and apportioned his ashes inside Kirkwall library's most execrable titles in the hope that when people ruffled or fluttered the pages, parts of him would waft up the readers' noses, causing them to sneeze and blast sputum across the books, and drop them (with luck in to a bin or bath), or even better, to cause a serious choking incident and bring the readers to an unpleasant quietus. It was a watered-down compromise of what he might have wanted. Sorting through Raine's papers, she found a manuscript called *Songs of the Sinner*, a complete novel. She broke open a box of wine and read the 400 pages in one sitting in her bed. "Oh Raine. You misheaded plonk of a man," she muttered to herself upon realising that Raine had written a masterpiece for his second novel and stuffed it in a cupboard pending the panning of *Broken Cello*. The reception to that novel would have made its follow-up unpublishable anyway, but the book should have been released. Isobel mailed the MS to one of the chief editors at Random House, with the message "Read this, prickhead!" attached. The man liked to be provoked. In two weeks, Raine's posthumous novel was released to worldwide acclaim, burying the works of Marcus T. Schott, which were soon forgotten. "At last, a real writer triumphs!" she yelled when she noticed Raine had killed everyone on the bestseller lists: translations of his novel occupied the first one hundred entries.

"Right, Marcustody, it's time to move to London. I intend to raise Funkadelic among the luminaries of the emerging Soho demimonde. You can read Boxallbrain in your study, while I find a more captive audience for my magnificence. Raine's royalties will pay for the enormous house we will occupy."

"OK," said Marcus.

"Right, Goddaddy, it's time to move to London. The political landscape of Westminster has shifted and self-loathing misanthropists with unfuckwithable moral frameworks are running the show. You can enter the cabinet straight away."

"OK," said Thorfin.

"And, before we go, one final thing to honour Raine: hey, reader! Yes, you! Fuck you, you illiterate, lazy, indifferent, unappreciative, changeable, moaning, ill-read, self-obsessed, zombie fuckwad. Sorry, but, that's also what he would have wanted."

On Reading

Final Fucking Lesson

"READ WIDELY, motherfuckers," I said, noting the workshop responded to my fucking swearing. "Launch yourselves into bookstores, conglomerate or otherwise, and pounce upon any and every fucking book that takes your fancy, and any and every fucking book that doesn't. Find your own fucking books. Fuck the university syllabus, the Peter fucking Boxall lists, *The Guardian*'s Top 100 since 1900, the lists of online fucking know-it-alls. Compile your own fucking lists using your own sense of whatever the fuck makes you giddy. Pick books based on fucking titles, fucking covers, fucking opening lines, fucking smartass hipster friends, and read the fuckers until you have a handle on this fucking shit. Don't fucking sit there in your comfy fucking pants, flicking through the same same-old bullshit, I said read fucking *widely*, motherfuckers. Read books so beyond your level of cognisance, you might as well be reading Sanskrit. Read novels in fucking Sanskrit. Read novels never intended to be read by you, because you fucking can. Be a promiscuous bastard. Fuck the fuck out of books. Fuck them again and again, come hard on their mangled spines. And when you think you can't take another fucking sentence of this literary fucking shit, fuck more words into your fucking eyes, fuck them into your fucking eyes until you are fucking blinded in the fucking face with bliss. Fucking READ, motherfuckers. READ."

Appendix: Spacey's Photographs

Images from
Poetry of the Lost: 103 Photographs by Spacey Vickers,
2018, Art Forum Press

Frog

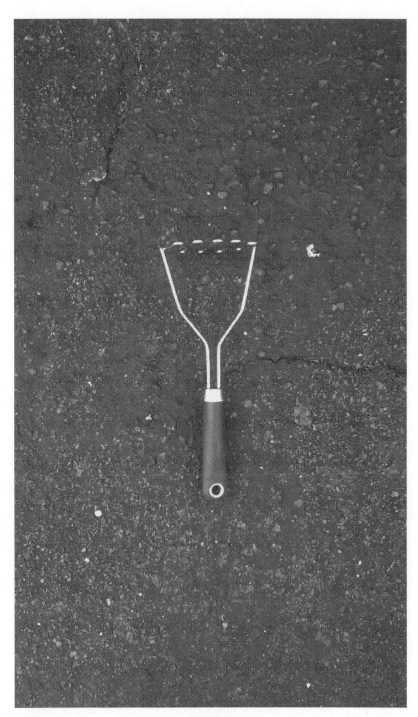

Masher

Sprout

Cup

Mushroom